RYAN'S CHRISTMAS

A DCI RYAN MYSTERY

LJ Ross

OTHER BOOKS BY LJ ROSS

The Alexander Gregory Thrillers in order:

1. *Impostor*
2. *Hysteria*
3. *Bedlam*

The DCI Ryan Mysteries in order:

1. *Holy Island*
2. *Sycamore Gap*
3. *Heavenfield*
4. *Angel*
5. *High Force*
6. *Cragside*
7. *Dark Skies*
8. *Seven Bridges*
9. *The Hermitage*
10. *Longstone*
11. *The Infirmary (prequel)*
12. *The Moor*
13. *Penshaw*
14. *Borderlands*
15. *Ryan's Christmas*

"By the pricking of my thumbs
Something wicked this way comes…"

—William Shakespeare, *Macbeth*

CHAPTER 1

The Friday before Christmas

"Hell's bells, I'm freezin' me nuts off in here!"

Detective Chief Inspector Maxwell Finlay-Ryan glanced at his sergeant in the rear-view mirror, then turned his attention back to the road ahead.

"The heating's already on full blast," he said, pulling a face at the temperature gauge, which confirmed it was below zero outside. Snow had been falling steadily ever since they'd left Edinburgh, and the journey back to Northumberland had been slow going. Normally, it was a pleasant two-hour drive but, judging by the worsening conditions outside, it would be a while longer before they made it home.

There followed a theatrical *brrr,* as Detective Sergeant Frank Phillips shook himself all over and rubbed his hands together.

"I *told* you to wear a thicker jumper, Frank. The forecast said there was a good chance of snow this weekend."

These wise words were spoken by Detective Inspector Denise MacKenzie, the other occupant in the back seat of Ryan's car, who also had the dubious honour of being Phillips' wife.

"It's not a jumper I need, it's a bit of winter padding," he replied, rubbing his belly. "It's this new-fangled diet you've had me on—"

"If you think 'reducing your bacon stottie intake' is *new-fangled,* I dread to think what you make of things like 'the wheel' and 'motorised tractors'," she drawled.

"Har har," he said. "You'll not be saying that, when you want to snuggle up later and find I'm nothing but skin and bones—"

Ryan hurriedly turned up the radio to drown out the rest of their conversation.

"Thank God," he said, as George Michael began to croon about having given someone his heart last Christmas. There were some things in life he didn't need to know about, and *snuggling* in the Phillips-MacKenzie household was one of them.

In the passenger seat beside him, his own better half, Anna, wrapped her arms around her chest and peered through the windscreen. It had seemed like a good idea to make a day trip to Edinburgh with their closest friends; to enjoy a rare moment of respite from the all-consuming work of fighting crime, in their case—and academic history, in hers. The foursome had spent a happy few hours wandering around the festive market nestled at the foot of Edinburgh Castle, laughing and nibbling toffee apples as they immersed themselves in the season of goodwill.

But now, as the city lights receded and the road stretched out in a blanket of white before them, she felt a moment's fear. It was after five, and darkness had fallen. Somewhere to the east, the North Sea crashed restlessly against the shore, while the stark landscape of the borderlands lay off to the west. Snow fell heavily as they wound their way through the gloomy landscape and the windscreen wipers swished back and forth to clear the gathering flakes.

Anna had been born in that far-flung corner of the world, on the tidal island of Lindisfarne, which was cut off from the mainland twice a day. Winters on the island had been harsh, with winds so penetrating they cut to the bone, and she knew that storms like these could set in quickly and take root for hours—sometimes days. The main road from Scotland hugged the rugged coastline and was therefore exposed to the worst of the elements; even now, the wind battered the side of their car, as though some pagan god had flicked it with the edge of their mighty finger. She cast a grateful eye towards Ryan, whose face was a hard mask of concentration as his hands steered a steady course over ground that was growing more treacherous by the minute.

As if he'd read her mind, Ryan reached across to lay a hand briefly over hers, which was curled tightly on her lap.

"Are you alright?" he murmured.

"I've seen storms like these before," she said quietly. "I think we should find somewhere to stop, until the worst of it passes."

Ryan opened his mouth to argue, then snapped it shut again. Visibility was reduced to a few feet, scarcely beyond the twin beams of his headlights, and he didn't dare go above thirty miles per hour or risk skidding into the path of oncoming traffic.

That's another thing, he realised.

There hadn't been any oncoming traffic for the last few miles.

"What does the GPS say?" he asked. "Is there somewhere nearby we could ride it out for an hour or two?"

Anna reached for her mobile, only to pause when a traffic update interrupted the track playing on the radio.

"This is BBC Radio Newcastle, and the time is ten past five. The Met Office has upgraded its previous weather warning from yellow to red for the

North East of England, as well as parts of Central Scotland and the Highlands. Extreme weather conditions are expected to set in over the coming hours, and travellers are advised to take action now to keep themselves safe. The A1 motorway will be closed in both directions between Berwick-upon-Tweed and Morpeth following an accident…"

Ryan swore softly. They had already passed Berwick some miles back, which meant the road must have closed sometime after.

"Keep a lookout for any signs of a diversion," he said. "There must be one coming up soon, unless we've already missed it."

Anna nodded, and MacKenzie leaned forward in her seat to speak to them both.

"Did I just hear something about the road being closed?"

Ryan nodded.

"What time do you need to be back to collect Samantha?"

He referred to the little girl Phillips and MacKenzie were in the process of adopting; a wiry, red-headed ten-year-old who had taken their lives by storm and stolen their hearts in the process.

"She's staying overnight at her friend's house," MacKenzie said, with some relief. "There's no need to rush on our account."

"No chance of rushing anywhere, more's the pity," Ryan said, and then narrowed his eyes against the white mist outside.

Flashing lights.

He slowed his car as a line of yellow hazard cones came into view. They stood across the breadth of the road, and illuminated arrows guided motorists towards a B-road leading off the dual carriageway, signposted for West Kyloe and Wooler.

Ryan glanced at the road behind them for any signs of life, but no other headlights emerged from the darkness and it was impossible to see whether there were any tyre tracks on the road ahead, which might have offered some encouragement that other drivers had passed that way before.

"If we can get to Wooler, there's bound to be a pub," Phillips said, in a voice laden with false cheer. "Might even have a bed for the night."

"It's getting there that's the problem," Ryan replied.

The road ahead was blocked, and he considered turning back in the direction they had come, but another strong gust of wind rocked the car and decided the matter for him. Away from the coast, they would at least be sheltered from the worst of the gale.

"Hold on to your nuts, Frank."

Carefully, he steered them off the main road and into the unknown.

CHAPTER 2

They might have been sheltered from the wind, but there was no shelter from the snow, which covered the county of Northumberland in a layer of white, obliterating the usual landmarks and road signs that might have guided their way.

"How long since we came off the A1?" Anna wondered aloud.

"Fifteen minutes," Ryan said, having already asked himself the same question. "There should have been another sign for Wooler by now. What does the map say?"

But there was no data signal in that part of the country, which was isolated, remote and surrounded by distant hills that loomed over them like sleeping giants.

"I can't get a signal," Anna replied. "But, from memory, I think we might have veered too far south."

There was a short, tense silence as they considered the implications of that. There had been some hairy moments since leaving the dual carriageway, with the car struggling to make it over the hidden peaks and troughs of the country lanes, skidding once or twice as an unexpected bend loomed out of the darkness. Roads that were usually so familiar and unthreatening seemed alien to them now, and filled with danger.

To make matters worse, they'd turned down a single-track road flanked with high hedgerows on either side and no hope of turning or reversing, should the need arise.

The only thing to do was forge ahead.

"If we've gone south, at least that's in the right direction," MacKenzie offered.

"Yes, and we can't be far from Chatton," Anna said, thinking of a large village with at least one pub—less than a mile away from where they crept through the snowy darkness, if they'd only known it.

Ryan checked the fuel gauge and a muscle ticked at the side of his jaw.

Ten-mile range.

He'd planned to top up the fuel at the petrol station in Alnwick, further down the A1, never imagining they'd be forced to take a seemingly endless diversion into the depths of the countryside.

"Ah…not to worry anybody, but we're low on fuel."

"That does it," Phillips said, throwing up his hands. "Next thing, you'll be telling me we've got a flat—"

He broke off as Ryan brought the car to a sudden emergency stop. Its rear end swung dangerously towards the hedge, and sent Phillips lurching against the car door with a soft thud.

It couldn't be helped, for standing in the middle of the road was the most unusual cow they'd ever seen.

* * *

As far as cattle went, this one was majestic.

Until it had been caught in the car's headlights, the cow had been well camouflaged, its downy coat an off-white colour that blended perfectly with the present climate.

"That's part of the Chillingham herd," Anna whispered, as if it could hear them.

"What does that mean?" Phillips whispered back.

"Wild cattle," she explained. "The rarest breed of cattle in the world, dating back to before the Domesday Book."

Realising she was surrounded by friends who didn't necessarily share her love of all things historical, she decided to elaborate.

"Their lineage goes all the way back to the thirteenth century," she said. "They exist without any interference from mankind— apart from chucking them the odd bale of hay, the park rangers don't even touch them, and nobody else is allowed to. They breed, live and die by the land."

"You said 'Chillingham'," Ryan said, focusing on the most important piece of information. "I've heard of the castle. Are the two connected?"

Anna turned to smile at him through the darkness.

"They're not only connected," she said, "the parkland where the cattle graze is in Chillingham village, across the road from the castle grounds. If that cow managed to break out, it can't have roamed far from home."

Four sets of eyes turned back to the road.

"That still doesn't solve our immediate problem," Ryan said. "How the hell are we going to get past it?"

Anna shook her head.

"I can tell which one of us grew up in the country," she said. "They're wild cattle, Ryan, which means they're frightened of cars and humans. Honk your horn and it'll run back the way it came."

"Or charge straight for us," Phillips said, ominously.

"Only one way to find out," Ryan replied, and leaned on the horn, which ricocheted around the silent countryside.

As it happened, the cow neither ran away nor charged, deciding instead to saunter back through a hole in the hedgerow to re-join its fellows.

"That was a close shave," Phillips muttered, and three sets of eyes turned towards him in disbelief.

"Frank, we face murderous criminals on a daily basis," Ryan said. "Surely you're not afraid of a fluffy moo-cow?"

Phillips held his ground, having had an unfortunate run-in with one of the cow's bovine cousins many years before.

"All I'm saying is, let's get going, before they find our frozen bodies out here in three weeks' time, half-mauled by the moo-cows."

* * *

Without any GPS signal—or the friendly jingle of a Christmas ballad on the radio, which had crackled and cut out shortly before their stand-off with the cow—it was another ten long minutes before they reached any sign of civilisation, which came in the form of a long, stone-built boundary wall.

"The castle must be over that wall, which means the village must be somewhere nearby," Ryan said, and dared to hope for a cup of coffee in the not-too-distant future.

"I don't remember there being much in the way of a village," Anna said, and was sorry to be the bearer of sad tidings. "It's mostly farmland and a few residential cottages and houses, I don't know about a pub or a hotel."

"Maybe somebody'll take pity on us," Phillips said.

"What about the castle?" MacKenzie asked.

"I think the castle is privately owned, but it has quite a few guest apartments where people can stay overnight," Anna said. "They run ghost tours—"

"Ghost tours?" Ryan said, with a healthy dose of scepticism.

"Mm hmm," she replied, and smiled at the look on his face. "It's known for being the most haunted castle in England."

"Well, that's just dandy, that is," Phillips muttered, and folded his arms across his burly chest. "It's not enough to be stranded out here in the snowy wilderness, or to survive a near-death experience with an angry bull…now you tell me there's poltergeists knockin' around the place!"

"We're not stranded just yet…" Ryan started to say, as the car suddenly coughed, spluttered, and came to a shuddering stop outside a set of enormous iron gates rising up from the darkness.

Ryan tried the ignition a couple of times, but the car refused to start.

"I guess the fuel gauge was wrong when it told me we still had another ten miles in the tank," he said, and twisted around in his seat to face the other three.

"Any clever ideas?"

"We must be close to the village, now," MacKenzie said. "Why don't we take a walk and see?"

"Have you seen the ground outside?" Phillips said, pressing his nose against the window. "Snow must be over a foot deep already, and, if it's cold in here with the heating on, it'll be bloody Arctic out there."

"Well, we can't stay here all night," Ryan told him.

"Look," Anna said softly, and pointed towards the gates. "There are lights in the windows of the castle."

They followed the direction of her gaze and saw that she was right. At the end of a long, sweeping driveway, they saw the distant glimmer of lights shining through the snowfall.

"Seems like the best option so far," Ryan said, and then cleared his throat. "There's only one problem."

He turned the ignition key to activate the headlights and illuminate the castle gates, which were easily twenty feet high to match the perimeter wall.

"They're padlocked," he said simply. "And, I don't know about you lot, but I don't fancy my chances of being able to scale that wall."

"Well, what are we goin' to do, then?" Phillips exclaimed.

"Find the back entrance," MacKenzie said, with her usual good sense. "There's bound to be one, a place this size."

They looked out into the shadowy night, and then at each other.

"I'll find it," Ryan offered, thinking of Denise's leg, which had been badly injured a couple of years before and was still a source of discomfort, especially in cold weather.

But MacKenzie had her pride.

"We'll all go," she told him.

"Aye, if there're any spooks about, we can't leave you to fend them off on your own," Phillips declared. "Howay, let's go and invade this castle."

CHAPTER 3

By the time they found the side entrance, their extremities were numb. It was located less than half a mile away from where they'd abandoned the car, but what might have been an easy walk in high summer was now a hazardous trail covered in snow and ice. They kept close to the boundary wall which ran parallel to the road, using the torch function on their phones to guide their way through the penetrating darkness until they arrived in front of a second, slightly smaller set of gates.

Only to find they were padlocked too.

"I don't believe this," Phillips muttered, and wrapped a supportive arm around MacKenzie's shoulders as they stood shivering in the frozen landscape.

Ryan tugged the chain, half hoping it was only for show, but the heavy iron links refused to budge. He blinked snowflakes from his eyes and looked down at the ground.

"Somebody's been out here recently," he called out. "I can see tyre tracks and footprints."

"Let's try the gatekeeper's lodge," Anna called back, and began trudging towards a nearby cottage, keeping her head bent against the driving snow which stung her cheeks.

No lights burned in the windows of the lodge, except for the faintest glow of a candle sitting on one of the sills. Anna had scarcely raised her fist to knock on the front door, when it swung open to reveal the silhouette of a man. He was tall and broad—at least as tall as Ryan, at well over six feet—and dressed for the weather in thick clothing and a padded waterproof jacket. They could see nothing of his face, having been blinded by the glaring light of the torch he raised to inspect each of them in turn.

"Lost?" he asked.

"Stranded," Ryan replied. "Our car's out of petrol, so we left it over by the main gates and hiked over here. We'd be grateful if you could shelter us for a while, and perhaps we could borrow your phone? None of us can get a signal on our mobiles, out here."

"No, you wouldn't in these parts," the man said, enigmatically. "You're welcome to come in, but there isn't much I can offer you, since the power line went down ten minutes ago."

That explains the lack of light, Anna thought.

"I'm the Estate Manager at the castle," the man continued. "I was about to head up there, myself. You're welcome to join me, and I'll drop you at the door."

Soon after, they found themselves ensconced in a battered Land Rover, and Phillips could only be glad that he'd resisted his wife's attempts to reduce his bacon consumption for, without the extra padding in his posterior, the lack of suspension would have done untold damage as they rattled through the side gates and up a winding, pot-holed driveway.

"How'd you find yourselves all the way out here, then?" the manager asked.

"There was a diversion from the A1," Ryan replied, blowing on his hands to warm them. "It was supposed to take us via Wooler or Chatton, but there were no signs and, like I say, we haven't any mobile signal."

The Estate Manager nodded, and Ryan turned to get a better look at him. Although he'd kept his hood up and wore a thick ski mask beneath it for warmth, the man's eyes were visible, and he'd have estimated from the fine lines fanning out on either side that he was somewhere in his fifties.

"Thanks for helping us out," Ryan said. "We were starting to run out of ideas, back there."

The man gave him a quick look, then turned back to the wheel.

"Aye, if you're not prepared for bad weather, it can be murder up here."

No pun was intended, but Phillips was amused, nonetheless.

"What's your name, mate?"

"Bill Dodds," he replied.

"Well you've narf saved our bacon, tonight, Bill. I thought they'd find me frozen solid out there, lookin' like Jack Nicholson in *The Shining.*"

MacKenzie wondered idly whether she should be worried about her husband's obsession with pork produce.

"It's no trouble," Dodds replied. "There's a few people staying at the castle already, so a couple more won't hurt."

"Oh? I hope we're not interrupting a family gathering?" Ryan asked.

"The family are visiting friends in the south for Christmas," Dodds explained. "The staff are looking after the place and dealing with the last of the guests this season. We were due to have a Candlelit Christmas Ghost Hunt this weekend, but the weather's put paid to that, I reckon."

"Do you think there'll be room for a few more?" MacKenzie asked, raising her voice above the roar of the engine as it fought its way over the snowy turf.

Dodds didn't answer directly, but looked amongst them, as if wondering for the first time whom he'd invited into the confines of his car.

"Where've you come from, anyhow?"

"Sorry, I should have introduced myself. I'm Maxwell Ryan, and this is my wife, Anna—and these are our friends, Frank Phillips and Denise MacKenzie. We were on our way back from Edinburgh when the storm hit."

"Came in quick," Dodds agreed. "Were you up there on business?"

"No, we're enjoying a couple of days off," Ryan said.

"Aye, the boss is a tyrant," Phillips chimed in, with a wink for MacKenzie.

"Watch yourself, Frank, or I might suddenly remember a stack of paperwork that needs filing before the twenty-fifth," Ryan said, wickedly.

Dodds smiled at their by-play.

"What line of work are you in?" he asked.

"The thin blue one," Anna replied. "They're all murder detectives, from Northumbria CID."

Dodds made a small sound of surprise behind the muffler on his face.

"Well, you've come to the right place," he said. "There must've been hundreds of murders committed up here, over the centuries. That's why so many ghosts roam around, haunting the living."

"Never fear, the Ghostbusters are here," Phillips said. "You just point us in the direction of Old Headless Harry, and we'll have a word with him for you."

The others laughed along, but Dodds grew serious.

"I know what people must think," he said quietly. "Most folk think it's nonsense, or that it's all staged to frighten people who'll believe anything. But, until you've seen it, or heard it for yourself…Just be careful what you wish for, that's all."

The car fell silent and its occupants turned their attention back to the passing scenery, having experienced a sudden chill that had very little to do with the weather. Dense woodland lined either side of the road, so thick they could see little more than the brief outline of ancient elm trees, whose eerie, twisted trunks had grown wild and free to form a loose arch above their heads. Ryan had a fleeting impression of being driven through some kind of portal; a tunnel from one world into another, where reality was not quite as it seemed, but he immediately dismissed the notion as ridiculous.

There was no such thing as ghosts.

Presently, they emerged from the thicket to find a vast, crenellated castle awaiting them on the other side. Its fortified walls stood tall and firm against the snow which pummelled it from every direction, and Dodds urged his Land Rover up to the entrance, which consisted of a set of gigantic, heavily-reinforced wooden doors at the top of a short flight of stone steps.

"Here we are," he said, and brought the car to a jerky stop at the foot of the stairs.

They followed him back into the blizzard, treading carefully as they mounted the icy steps leading up to the castle doors. Dodds produced a large iron key, and, after a moment they heard the lock click free and the heavy oak door began to creak open on rusted hinges.

Ryan looked over his shoulder, but there was nothing except snow and the vague outline of trees, as far as the eye could see. He gave himself a mental shake and turned back to find the others hurrying inside the protective fold of the castle's walls.

"Enter freely and of your own will," he muttered, and stepped over the threshold.

The door clanged shut behind him.

CHAPTER 4

Beyond the heavy oak doors, the castle had been built in a quadrangle formation, with a large inner courtyard giving access to each floor via a large central staircase and four smaller, spiral staircases located in each corner. The wind continued to howl the inside enclosed space, circling around the nooks and crannies like a banshee while the foursome huddled inside the entrance portico.

"What've we got here, then?"

A lady of indeterminate middle-age emerged from a side door, dressed in comfortable 'country' garb consisting of fleece-lined waterproof chinos and worn leather boots, a thick woollen jumper and gloves, accessorized by a padded jacket that covered her from neck to knee.

"Got a few weary travellers for you, Carole," Dodds said, giving her a peck on the cheek. "They've had a bit of bad luck and their car's stranded over by the main gates. They'll be needing a place to kip, for tonight at least. It might be best if I stayed here tonight as well, at least until the power's back on at the lodge."

"I'm sure I can rustle up a bed or two," she said, turning to them with a cheery smile. "I'm Carole Black, the housekeeper here at Chillingham. Come on inside and warm yourselves."

They followed her through a door immediately to their right, bearing a smart plaque that said, 'ESTATE OFFICE'. It was a cosy, cluttered space, warmed by several storm heaters placed around the room and to which they were immediately drawn in an effort to thaw their frozen bones. The remaining space consisted of two large desks, several filing cabinets, notice boards and various other odds and ends that were no doubt integral to the running of such a large establishment, and a good deal more besides.

Dodds moved to his desk at the back of the room and began unwrapping the layers of clothing he wore, revealing a well-built, ruddy-faced man of around sixty—older than Ryan had first imagined, but with a youthful demeanour that belied his years.

"We're sorry to put you to any trouble," he said, to the room at large. "It's been a bit of a nightmare journey, so we're glad to have a roof over our heads."

Carole looked up from where she was rooting around her desk drawer for a set of apartment keys and gave him a sunny smile.

"Oh, don't mention it! You won't find a sturdier roof than here," she said, and then pulled an apologetic face. "I'm afraid all the best rooms are already occupied; we were due to host a Candlelit Ghost Hunt this evening with a meal beforehand, and most guests managed to get here before the snow set in. There *are* a couple of apartments you can use in the north-west tower which should be very comfortable—"

"We're grateful for anything you can offer us," Anna said quickly.

"That's settled, then. Of course, you're very welcome to join us in the Great Hall for dinner at eight," Carole said, and checked the time on her watch. "It's almost six, now, so I should be getting along to the kitchen. Normally, we have a chef who lives in, but he's away visiting family and the stand-in hasn't been able to make it through the snow."

They looked among themselves.

"We'll lend a hand, if you need it?" MacKenzie offered. "It's the least we can do—"

"Oh, no, no. That's kind, but I like my time pottering in the kitchen and, besides, I have Mr Black to help me," she said. "If you'd like to sign the guest book, I'll show you around."

"Tomorrow morning, we can try to tow your car," Dodds put in, while they each took it in turns to scrawl their names in a leather-bound book. "I've got a bit of fuel I keep for the quad bikes and the Land Rover—I can siphon some off and try to get you going again, once the snow lets up."

"That'd be much appreciated," Phillips told him. "Y' know, confidentially, this would never've happened if we'd taken my Volvo—"

MacKenzie snorted from the other side of the room.

"If you'd been driving, we'd have probably ended up in a snowdrift," she said, roundly.

Phillips didn't bother to argue, since she was probably right.

"Do you mind if I make a quick phone call?" Ryan asked, once the formalities had been completed.

"Lines are down, over at the lodge," Dodds said, turning to Carole. "What're they like up here?"

"We had a bit of a wobble with the lights, but they came back on, so the cables must be holding up, so far. I haven't tried the phone line," Carole replied. "Why don't you try the one on my desk?"

Ryan moved around to pick up the handset and, when he heard the dial tone in his ear, gave them all a thumbs-up.

A couple of seconds passed, then his voice rang out into the expectant room.

"This is DCI Ryan," he recited his badge number. "Can you put me through to Chief Constable Morrison, please?"

Ryan caught the startled look which passed between the Housekeeper and the Estate Manager, and wondered about it. Then again, people tended to get nervous at the very mention of police, even when they'd done nothing wrong.

"Ma'am? This is Ryan. I wanted to let you know that there's a chance that Phillips, MacKenzie and I may not be back into the office by Monday."

From her desk back at Northumbria Police Headquarters, Sandra Morrison raised her eyebrows.

"Oh, yes? Far be it for me to remind you, but we have a fair amount on the books at this time of year. Now isn't the time to scamper off for a jolly—"

"I realise that, ma'am, and I'm sorry for the inconvenience but I'm afraid it can't be helped. We ran into some trouble on the road back from Edinburgh today, and we've taken shelter at Chillingham Castle."

"I heard the snow was bad up near the Borders, but I hadn't realised it was *that* bad," she admitted. "Well, just get back as soon as you can."

"We're hoping things might clear up by tomorrow, but it doesn't look good, so far."

"Understood. Take care of yourselves—and, Ryan?"

"Ma'am?"

"Try not to get into any trouble."

* * *

Reluctantly, they left the relative warmth of the Estate Office and braved the open courtyard, their boots sinking into a fresh layer of snow as they hurried towards the north-west tower and followed Carole up a narrow flight of spiral steps.

"Here's your apartment," she said, panting a little as they reached the top. "We call it 'The Lookout'."

They could see why, for it was just below the uppermost rafters of the castle and would likely have far-ranging views of the parkland and gardens to the west, once the snow cleared.

"This is one of the oldest parts of the castle, dating back to the thirteenth century, and I'm afraid it has the draughts to prove it," Carole said, turning on all the radiators. "We weren't expecting to use this apartment, or I'd have made sure it was ready for you."

"We'll manage just fine," Ryan said, eyeing the small kitchen which boasted a kettle and, better yet, a jar of coffee sitting beside it.

"There are two double bedrooms through there, and the bathroom's next door. I'll send Bill or one of the others up with some spare pyjamas and towels," she said. "If you need anything else, just use the internal telephone and dial the number for the Estate Office. Dinner will be in the Great Hall, which is up the main stairs across the courtyard. You can't miss it. Feel free to explore the castle until then—the only area which is out of bounds is the Dungeon in the north-eastern corner of the castle. We're repairing the wall of the oubliette, so it's roped off at the moment."

"Oubliette?" Mackenzie asked.

Carole smiled. "I think the word has a French origin, something to do with 'forgetting'. The oubliette is basically a pit in the corner of the dungeon where they used to throw the prisoners and forget about them. There's a guidebook on the coffee table through there if you want to learn more about the castle's history."

She turned to go, but then paused to look back.

"Sometimes… people say they *hear* things in the castle," she said, with a touch of embarrassment. "It probably sounds silly, to those who don't live here."

Wisely, they said nothing.

"People also complain of being nudged in the back, or of having their hair pulled," she continued. "I don't want to scare you, only—just be careful. The staircases are steep in the castle, and there are plenty of them. I wouldn't want to see any of you taking a tumble."

Suddenly, she was all smiles again.

"I'll see you at eight."

In the brief silence that followed her departure, Phillips turned to the others and spoke in an undertone, as if the walls might hear him.

"You know, I'm getting an awful funny feeling that we might have fallen out of the fryin' pan and straight into the fire."

Right on cue, the mullioned windows shook as a strong gust of wind battered the western wall and burst through its cracks with a long whine, like that of a soul in torment.

Ryan moved across to draw the heavy brocade curtains and caught sight of a single beam of light hovering in the gardens far below.

"You know what, Frank? I've a funny feeling you might be right."

CHAPTER 5

The Great Hall proved true to its name.

It was an impressive long gallery, built sometime during the sixteenth century to link the ancient towers on the south-eastern and south-western corners of the castle, in preparation for a visit from the Scottish King James VI. A hearty fire crackled in the grate of its enormous chimneypiece and polished silver candelabra illuminated a banqueting table in the centre of the room, the candlelight flickering against the faces of those who had already taken their place at the feast. There were six in total; four women and two men, by Ryan's count, and each of them turned to stare at the new arrivals with open curiosity.

"Ah, you found us, then!"

Carole Black, whose diminutive figure had been partially obscured behind a full suit of armour, crossed the room to greet them.

"A shower and a cuppa revived us," Phillips said, in his easy way.

"Everybody, if I can have your attention for a moment, we have some late arrivals joining us this evening," Carole said. "This is Mr and Mrs Ryan, and Mr and Mrs Phillips."

Anna and Denise exchanged an eloquent look, each woman wondering why they'd bothered to retain any semblance of their own identity after marriage, if they would forever be referred to as 'the missus'.

"This here's Mr and Mrs Enfield," Carole said, indicating a jovial looking pair in their early sixties, seated at one end of the table. "In the middle here, we have Mrs Baker and her daughter," she continued, nodding at two women in their early sixties and early thirties, respectively. "Finally, this is Mr Sage and Miss Halliwell."

The latter raised her champagne glass in a parody of 'cheers' and downed the bubbling liquid in one gulp.

Seemingly from nowhere, a butler materialised from the shadows to refill it.

"This is my husband, Samuel," Carole said. "We work together."

Unlike his wife, the man was tall and reed-thin, dressed in the ubiquitous uniform of black waistcoat and tails. He was of a similar age to his wife, being somewhere in his late fifties, and was possessed of a quiet, watchful manner that contrasted with her more expansive demeanour.

Places had been set for them in pairs of two at either end of the table, so the foursome separated and resigned themselves to an evening making awkward small talk with their nearest neighbours. Whilst Phillips approached this much as he would a wedding reception—namely, with extroverted gusto—Ryan was forced to bank down his naturally misanthropic tendencies and school his features into some semblance of a smile.

Whether they'd drawn the short straw, they couldn't say, but Ryan and Anna found themselves seated beside the older couple, who re-introduced themselves as Sheila and David Enfield and didn't pause to draw breath until after the first course of scallops had been served.

"—anyhow, I said to David, I said, we *have* to come this weekend. Didn't I, Dave?"

The question was rhetorical, and apparently her husband knew it, for he continued to chew on a piece of soda bread while making murmuring sounds of agreement in his throat.

"The gift voucher was all expenses paid, which is nothing to sniff at, is it? How about you two? You know, I've got a son around your age," she said, patting Ryan's arm. "Wish he'd get married and give me some grand-babies. Do you two have children?"

She looked between the pair of them with wide, myopic eyes, as if it were completely normal to enquire into the personal affairs of people she had never met in her life before.

"Sheila," her husband chided. "Leave this poor couple to eat their dinner. They must be famished, after the journey they've had."

Ryan shot him a grateful look, and Anna continued to stare at her plate, blinking rapidly.

"Oh, alright, alright. You know I don't mean anything by it," she said, waving around a breadstick. "I like to get to know people, that's all. Did you find your way here by accident, or did you have a voucher, too?"

"We came here by accident," Ryan confirmed, in a clipped, well-rounded tone his staff would have recognised immediately as a warning that he was nearing the end of his tether. "We were caught in the snowstorm, on our way south along the A1."

"Oh, yes, I think we just missed it," one of the other women chimed in, from Sheila's other side. "We managed to get in just as the snow started coming down hard, which is good because I don't have a four-wheel drive."

She went on to introduce herself as Jacqui Baker, and her daughter, Rosie.

"I've never been to a ghost hunt before, have you?"

"No, but Ryan's always wanted to, haven't you, darling?"

Anna gave him an innocent look, and sipped her wine, eyes glinting at him.

"I often speak of little else," he replied.

"You must be so *excited!*" Sheila Enfield exclaimed. "Have you ever communed with the dead?"

Ryan searched her face for any sign that she was joking, but could find none.

He cleared his throat.

"C—communed? No, can't say that I have," he replied. "Anna's heard a few things go bump in the night, mind you."

The smile he sent his wife could only be described as roguish.

"Don't feel too bad," Sheila said. "Some people have the gift, others don't."

"Thank you," Ryan said, gravely.

"We're planning a séance after dinner," she continued. "Maybe you'll get lucky and hear something."

"With you there beside me, Mrs Enfield, I'm sure I will."

* * *

At the other end of the table, Phillips was already cursing whichever higher power had decided to seat him next to Miss Halliwell—or *Nadia,* as she'd asked him to call her—and was growing increasingly hot under the collar beneath the scrutiny of his wife, who watched the young woman's antics from the other side of the table with a mixture of indulgence and irritation.

"You look like a strong man, Mr Phillips," Nadia said, and leaned in to gesture with her wine glass. "I bet you work with your hands."

He almost choked on a scallop and wondered frantically whether Ryan had to deal with this kind of thing all the time, looking like he did. Women liked 'Tall, Dark and Handsome', didn't they? That was the way of the world, wasn't it? Until this evening, he'd thought his wife was the only woman alive who went for, 'Short, Balding and Comfortably Rounded', but it took all sorts.

"Actually, I'm a police sergeant," he said, sternly.

"Do you get to wear a uniform?" she slurred.

Before Phillips could think of a polite response, Marcus Sage spoke in a voice so soft they strained to hear him above the snap and crackle of the fire at their backs.

"Eat your dinner, Nadia. You've had too much to drink on an empty stomach."

The words were plain and simple, but there was a tone to them that MacKenzie didn't like. Her body reacted to it like a wary animal, and the hairs on the back of her neck prickled. Unconsciously, she angled herself away from him, and took a hasty sip of water.

Apparently, Nadia had noticed it, too, because she fell silent and began to play with her food.

"Did you say you were with the police?" Sage continued.

Phillips nodded.

"I'm Detective Sergeant Frank Phillips, and this is my boss in all things, Detective Inspector Denise MacKenzie."

Sage laughed softly.

"It's a wise man who knows what side his bread's buttered," he said. "Tell me, detectives, are you hoping to catch any criminals here, this evening?"

"Why?" MacKenzie drawled. "Do you know any?"

Before he could answer, Nadia reached for her wine glass and managed to knock it over, spilling amber liquid all over the table.

"Sorry!" she mumbled, and tried to mop up the damage with her napkin, managing to bobble Phillips' water glass in the process. "Let me—I'll just—"

Samuel Black materialised again with a cloth in hand.

"No more wine for her," Sage snapped, and the butler inclined his head.

Once their plates had been cleared and the main course served, conversation picked up again, this time helped along by Rosie Baker, who had grown tired of hearing about the Enfields' past ghost-hunting exploits.

"Mrs Black was saying we could still do a mini ghost tour of the castle interior," she said. "Have any of you done one before?"

"Can't say that I have, love," Sage muttered. "It's just a bunch of hidden microphones and tricks of the light, isn't it?"

"Don't you think the spirits of the dead sometimes get trapped, here on Earth? What about all the people who say they've seen them?"

"Probably had one too many, the night before," he said, with a pointed look towards his girlfriend, who looked as though she might slide from her chair at any moment.

"What about you two?" Rosie asked.

Phillips and MacKenzie looked at one another, never having discussed the topic before.

"It isn't so much that I believe in ghosts," MacKenzie said slowly. "I don't think there are white effigies floating around, or anything like that. It's more of a psychological thing. In my work as a murder detective, I've seen what one person is capable of doing to another. I've seen the way people die, and that's a kind of haunting. The faces of the dead play on my mind and in my nightmares, until they're avenged."

There was a brief silence as her words began to sink in, and Phillips reached across the table to give her hand a quick squeeze, in solidarity.

"Once you die, you die," Sage argued. "I don't believe in any hocus pocus, and I don't waste my time worrying about them, once they're six feet under. The dead don't remember, they aren't around anymore to care about how or why they died, so why dwell on it?"

Phillips set his knife and fork down carefully, and leaned back in his chair.

"You don't think the dead deserve justice? What about their families?"

"It won't bring them back, will it?"

"No, it doesn't bring them back, but it might help their loved ones sleep soundly at night."

Sage lifted a negligent shoulder.

"That's their look-out."

CHAPTER 6

Ryan had seen a great many things over the years, but a séance was not one of them.

After a long dinner, during which he'd learned almost all there was to know about Sheila and David Enfield—including their voting tendencies and religious inclinations—he'd almost begun to wonder whether he'd been too hasty in dismissing the car as a viable place to spend the night, when their hostess announced that it was time to try to make contact with the spirits.

"I've heard it all, now," he muttered, as they followed the other guests into a smaller sitting room where the candles had already been lit at a circular table. "Can't we make a quick getaway down the back stairs?"

Anna grinned.

"Oh, go on," she urged him. "What harm can it do?"

Ryan stopped dead suddenly and swung around, eyes searching the passageway behind him.

"What?" she said urgently. "What is it?"

"Did you hear that?" he whispered, clutching her hand.

"Hear what?" she said, edging a little closer.

"Listen," he said softly.

Anna strained to hear anything beyond the rattle of the windowpanes and the burning embers of the fire.

"I still can't—"

He grabbed her waist and nuzzled her neck so that she let out an undignified squeal.

"You scared the living daylights out of me!"

Ryan burst out laughing and drew her in for a kiss.

"Just getting into the *spirit* of things," he said, and she gave him a playful jab to the ribs.

"If anything ever happens to me, I want you to know that I'm coming back to haunt you."

"Promise?"

* * *

Eleven people seated themselves around the table, which had been laid with a long damask cloth and a single candle in the middle. Dim lighting fizzed from old brass sconces, casting shadows on the walls and against the old weaponry and stuffed animal heads that watched them with glassy eyes.

"Who would like to go first?"

Carole Black was no longer the housekeeper now, but a medium; a woman accustomed to the occult. She was also adept at reading human behaviour, and would have been able to recognise the cynics in the room, even if Ryan *hadn't* been sitting with his arms folded in a classic 'closed' stance with his face set into lines of what she liked to call 'polite disbelief'. He was too well brought up to be openly disagreeable, but every fibre of his logical being told him it was a load of old hogwash.

They'd see if he felt the same by the end of it all.

"I'll go first," Jacqui Baker said, and pulled a comical face as if to say she was nervous. "What do I need to do?"

"We need a pendulum," Carole said. "Do you have a wedding ring, or a necklace—anything else that's personal to you?"

Jacqui pulled off her wedding ring and held it carefully in her hand, before handing it over.

"Don't lose it, will you?"

"I'll be very careful," Carole said, and knew immediately that this woman had loved her husband deeply.

She threaded a long piece of string through the tarnished gold hoop and then dunked it in a small cup of salty water.

"This is supposed to 'cleanse' the pendulum," she explained, drying it off on the edge of a napkin. "It won't damage the metal at all."

Jacqui nodded.

"The next thing is to think carefully about who you're hoping to speak to, on the other side," Carole said. "Don't tell anyone, keep it to yourself for now."

The detectives in the room exchanged a knowing glance. Easy enough to find out a little advance information about guests who were due to be staying at the hotel; it was the oldest trick in the book.

"Now," she said. "Let us join hands."

Ryan took Anna's hand, to his left, and MacKenzie's, to his right; Phillips held her other hand, and Rosie Baker's on his right, while the girl held her mother's left hand. Jacqui held David Enfield on her right side, who linked hands with Sheila. Marcus Sage was seated on Sheila's other side, and Nadia was held upright by him and Anna, to complete the circle.

Carole Black stood slightly apart, holding the pendulum aloft, and her husband kept to the back of the room to watch.

"What I need to make very clear is that this is a positive space," she said, in the soft candlelight. "There is no room here for negative energy. Is that understood?"

They all nodded.

"It's also important that we stay as quiet and as still as possible. Is that alright? Very well, let's begin."

She closed her eyes, took a couple of deep breaths in and out, then opened them again. She held the pendulum above the flame and waited until it was very still before speaking again.

"Pendulum, show us 'yes'."

It took a couple of seconds, and then the suspended wedding ring began to move in a clockwise motion.

"Pendulum, show us 'no'."

Slowly, it began to turn anti-clockwise.

"That's incredible," Sheila Enfield said, in a stage whisper.

Carole drew in another long breath.

"Is there anyone here who wishes to speak with us?"

They watched as the pendulum began to move clockwise around the candle's flame.

"Thank you, spirits," Carole whispered, while Ryan drew upon every ounce of his breeding and good manners to maintain a straight face.

"In life, were you male?"

The pendulum continued to spin clockwise, while Jacqui paled visibly. They went through a lengthy process of eliminating the letters of the alphabet until the pendulum swung clockwise when asked if the spirit's name began with an 'S'.

"Stuart!" Jacqui gasped. "Ask him—ask him if he's alright—"

Ryan didn't like this turn of events, and was about to say as much, when Carole suddenly gasped and her eyes took on a glazed expression as the pendulum began to swing wildly.

"He says there's another here who wishes to make herself known," she said, in an odd, faraway voice.

They went through the same process of elimination, until the pendulum turned clockwise around the letter 'E'.

"Does anyone here know of a spirit whose name begins with the letter 'E'?" Carole asked, looking around the table.

But nobody spoke up.

Carole proceeded to go through the alphabet again, until the full name was revealed as 'ELIZABETH'.

"Does anybody recognise an 'Elizabeth' who has passed on to the other realm?"

Ryan cast his eyes around, noting the different expressions on the faces of his fellow guests, all of whom shook their heads decisively.

"Very well," Carole said. "Spirit, we thank you, but fear you are in the wrong place—"

Just then, the pendulum began to spin anti-clockwise, forming wide circles around the flame.

No! it seemed to shout. *No, I'm not!*

"I've never seen anything like it," Carole said, in a hushed voice. "Elizabeth, do you mean us any harm?"

The pendulum continued to swing anticlockwise.

"Who have you come to see?"

D-R-A-G-F-O-O-T

The assembly looked at each other in confusion, never having heard of such a person. But the worst was yet to come.

"Why are you here?

Through the same process as before, the pendulum spelled out a single word.

M-U-R-D-E-R.

CHAPTER 7

The four friends in the room knew, much more than most, that murder was not something to be made light of, nor the subject of any parlour game. Whilst he had been content to play along, so long as the game remained harmless, now Ryan dropped his hands from the circle and stood up to turn on the overhead light, breaking the spell that had been woven—around some of them, at least.

"I think that's enough for one night, don't you?"

Carole blinked, as if coming out of a trance.

"I-I'm sorry, that's never happened before," she said.

Ryan wasn't about to enter into a fruitless discussion about whether or not that was true. He knew that murder would always be a source of intrigue to some; that explained the fictional crime series on television, the true-crime documentaries and novels written around the topic. But, to him, it was his profession—more than that, his *vocation* to advocate for the dead. It involved long, antisocial hours dealing with the worst of humanity, coming face to face with the destruction one person could inflict upon another. He met the families of those who had died and knew that their grief ran bone-deep. It made them vulnerable and credulous, sometimes willing to accept any kind of help if it came with the promise of communicating with their loved one, just one more time.

Ryan dealt in facts and evidence, tempered by compassion. He didn't offer false hope, no matter how sorely he was tempted.

"Usually, the pendulum only responds to its owner," Carole was saying. "I've never had a pendulum be overtaken by a spirit unconnected with its owner."

"The message must have been important," Sheila said, with rising excitement. "I wonder who Elizabeth was, and why she wants to kill Dragfoot?"

As they continued to talk, Anna walked around the table to where Jacqui Baker still sat looking shell-shocked, while her daughter sat quietly beside her, rubbing slow circles on her back and murmuring soft sounds of condolence.

"Are you alright?" she asked gently.

"It was—it was when she said 'S' for 'Stuart'," Jacqui replied, in a trembling voice. "He was my husband, you see. He died eight years ago."

"I'm sorry," Anna said, hardly able to imagine life without her love sleeping beside her each night.

"It was the best thing for him, really," Jacqui said tightly, and then held a hand over her eyes. "I don't mean that, really. I only mean that Stuart was in a very bad way, just before he died. We'd had some catastrophic news that changed our lives, and he couldn't quite cope with the stress of it all."

Anna didn't need to ask how he'd died, but Rosie answered the unspoken question anyway.

"My dad killed himself," she said. "He lost all their money on a bad investment. He wasn't the only one; there were hundreds of others in the same boat, but none of them ever got anything back. He blamed himself."

"I'm so sorry."

Rosie shook her head.

"It's as mum says. He's in a better place, now."

"I wanted to do the séance," Jacqui said. "I volunteered for it. I just didn't think—I never imagined it would actually *work*."

Anna held her tongue, deeming it an unkindness to try to argue otherwise. In the darkest moments of despair, people needed their beliefs to cling to, whatever they may be.

* * *

Later, when Marcus had escorted an inebriated Nadia back to the 'Grey Apartment', and the Enfields stayed a while longer chatting to the Baker women, the four friends bade them goodnight and thanked their hosts before beating a hasty retreat to The Lookout. After the warmth of the Great Hall, it came as a shock when they stepped back outside into the frozen night, the cold hitting them like a wall.

It came as an even greater shock when the clock above the entrance to the castle let out a clanging chime, to signal the hour.

Eleven o'clock.

"I bet they can hear that over in Newcastle!" Phillips exclaimed. "I hope it isn't going to do that every hour."

"I have a feeling it's going to," MacKenzie said. "Mind you, I'm so tired, I could sleep through a marching band."

"I'm a bit unsettled by that séance," Phillips admitted. "How could Carole have known that Jacqui's husband's name began with an 'S'?"

"Easy," Ryan replied, and locked the apartment door behind them. "She's the housekeeper, so she has access to a list of all the guests due to stay for the weekend. With that kind of advance information, all she has to do is a few searches online to find the name of Jacqui's husband. She probably knows something about all of the guests."

"Apart from us," Phillips said.

"I wouldn't be so sure. She might have recognised one or two of us from the local papers, or could have done a quick bit of research online. If she'd asked me to have a go, we'd have probably found a spirit whose name begins with the letter 'N', for Natalie."

He referred to his late sister, who had been murdered five years before at the brutal hands of a madman. Ryan had tried and failed to save her, and would have to live with that knowledge for the rest of his life.

Anna curled an arm around his waist and held him close, feeling the sadness rolling off him in waves.

"I thought it would be a bit of silly fun, but it wasn't. I'm sorry I suggested that we join in."

Ryan shook his head and pressed a kiss to her temple.

"You weren't to know it would take that kind of turn," he said. "It could just as easily have been a bit of light-hearted fun."

"Speaking of fun, what do you make of our fellow guests?" MacKenzie asked, as she filled the kettle to boil. "At one stage, I thought Frank was about to combust with embarrassment."

"I was *mildly* taken aback," Phillips said, with dignity.

"Nadia took a fancy to him," MacKenzie enlightened them. "Frank didn't know what to do with himself."

"The lass is half my age!"

"Since when has being with a younger woman ever held you back?" Ryan said, with a wink for MacKenzie, who was ten years his sergeant's junior.

"Oh aye, both of you gang up on me, why don't you? It was clear to see she'd had one too many glasses of the bubbly, that's all."

"You can say that again," MacKenzie sniffed. "I'm sure she'll have a thumping headache in the morning."

"Well, if it makes you feel any better, Sheila Enfield took quite a shine to Ryan," Anna said, as they settled on the sofas with mugs of tea.

"That was entirely different," Ryan said. "She said I reminded her of her own son."

"Mm hmm—if her son was 6'2", with black hair and blue-grey eyes."

"She's got you there, son. Just accept that you're afflicted by a pretty face and move on. That's what I do," Phillips grinned, and stroked his stubbled jaw to make them all laugh.

"Snow hasn't let up at all," MacKenzie said, rising to peek behind the curtains. "I can't see us getting out of here tomorrow morning, at this rate."

"Let's see what tomorrow brings," Ryan said. "Maybe the weather will change overnight."

CHAPTER 8

T hanks to the hourly chiming of the castle clock, the foursome gave up on any pretence of sleep shortly before eight. To make matters worse, one of the mullioned windows had burst open sometime during the night, and the wind whipped through the bedrooms to wake them with an icy kiss.

Phillips rushed to close it, wearing a pair of blue flannel pyjamas loaned to him by the Estate Manager, Bill Dodds, which were far too long in the leg and flapped around his ankles as he struggled against the force of the gale.

Once the latch was safely back in place, he saw what they'd all been hoping for.

Blue skies.

"The snow's packed in, at last!"

The others hurried to join him at the window and looked out at the bright new day. The clouds had emptied themselves, covering the land with snow so that it was truly a winter wonderland, but the wind had blown it into drifts that were several feet deep—which did not bode well for their journey home.

"Do you think we'll be able to dig out the car?" MacKenzie asked, though she feared she already knew the answer.

Ryan shook his head.

"I can't see us getting out of here, today," he said. "The car will be snowed under, even if we can get a vehicle down there to tow it out, which I doubt."

"Well, there are worse places to be, than stuck inside this beautiful castle," Anna said, valiantly masking her own disappointment. "We'll just have to brave the ghosts for another day, that's all."

At the thought of another lengthy conversation with Sheila Enfield, Ryan wondered whether it would be bad form to suggest calling in Mountain Rescue.

Probably.

"I'm with Anna on this one," Phillips declared. "We should settle in and think of this as an impromptu mini-break, starting with a full English breakfast."

"Hard to argue with that kind of logic," Ryan said. "There's just one problem."

"Which is?"

"We have no clean clothes."

"Ah, just turn your pants inside out," Phillips suggested, much to his wife's disgust. "That'll give you another day's wear."

"*Or,* I could call the Estate Office and see if we can scrounge some more clothes and a couple of spare toothbrushes."

"Well, if you want to get picky about it," Phillips mumbled, leaving MacKenzie to wonder what manner of man she had married.

It was lucky he was Short, Balding and Comfortably Rounded, that was for sure.

* * *

Breakfast was served in the smaller dining room, not far from the Great Hall in the south-eastern wing of the castle. They took a seat at its circular table, which appeared vastly different with sunlight streaming onto its polished surface and far less sinister than it had during the séance the previous evening. The kitchen was a couple of floors below, and was the domain of Carole Black, who bustled around frying bacon and toasting bread in the absence of their usual resident chef, while her husband served it all up to their guests.

"Can I get you some tea or coffee?"

It might have been the first time they'd heard Samuel Black speak, and they found his voice to be an unusual blend of Scots and English, unique to the borderlands. He didn't stop to chat after he'd taken their order, but moved on to the Enfields, who were already tucking into bowls of steaming porridge. Bill Dodds entered the room shortly afterwards, bearing the cold-tinged look of one who had been up with the larks.

"Morning, all," he said, helping himself to a slice of toast. "It looks nice out there, but the wind is still pretty brisk, I can tell you."

He stopped to spread a thick layer of jam on his toast and took a healthy bite.

"I wouldn't advise any of you to spend too long outside, unless you've got a thermal coat and a pair of proper boots," he said, between mouthfuls. "This isn't city weather; we're dealing with snowdrifts up to my waist, in some places."

"D'you think there's any chance of us getting back on the road today?" MacKenzie asked. She'd already called Samantha from the Estate Office, but was loathe to trespass too much longer on the generosity of her school friend's family.

Dodds shook his head.

"I can't open the garage doors, let alone get out there to tow your car. Sorry."

The four nodded and told themselves to accept the things they could not change.

A short time later, Dodds excused himself and passed Nadia Halliwell in the doorway, who wandered into the room wearing sunglasses and a designer jumpsuit that was entirely impractical for present conditions.

"I've got a few nice thermals you can borrow if you like, dear?" Sheila Enfield offered, feeling cold just looking at her.

Nadia made a non-committal sound and sauntered over to a spare seat.

"Coffee, please," she said in a croaky voice, when the butler made his rounds. "Marcus will have a coffee, too—he'll be up in a minute."

"You must be feeling a bit delicate today," Sheila continued, undeterred by the fact their conversation was mostly one-sided. "I've got some paracetamol in my wash bag, if you need it."

"Thanks," Nadia muttered. "I think I had one too many last night, and I hadn't had much to eat all day."

Sheila clucked her tongue.

"Have yourself a nice bit of toast, a strong cup of tea, and you'll feel better soon enough."

"Either that, or the hair of the dog," Anna said blithely.

Further conversation was interrupted by the chiming of the castle clock, followed by the sound of a piercing scream from somewhere outside.

Ryan was out of his chair first.

He crossed the room in a couple of paces to look out of the window, where he saw what he'd been dreading since the first moment he'd stepped over the castle's threshold.

It was Carole Black's twisted body, lying motionless in the snow.

CHAPTER 9

As he raced down the stone steps towards the nearest exit, Ryan's only thought was that it was impossible for Carole Black to be dead. He'd made a quick scan of the vicinity and noticed one indisputable fact. There had only been one set of snowy footprints leading from the kitchen out into the garden—and they could only belong to Carole.

He didn't stop to worry about that now, but continued to race through the castle with the thundering clatter of footsteps at his heels, through the main doors on the south wall and out into the bracing wind, but he found that he was not the first to arrive at the scene.

Marcus Sage and Rosie Baker stood beside Carole's inert body; Rosie having emptied the contents of her stomach in the snow nearby.

When he spotted Ryan emerging from the kitchen door, Sage began to wave frantically.

"Help! Over here! She's been stabbed!"

Ryan ran across the snow in a wide arc, to preserve whatever might be left of Carole's original tracks and was met with three pale faces—only one of which was dead.

"She—" Marcus gulped. "I think Carole's been stabbed."

Ryan took one look at the woman's lifeless eyes and nodded.

"Have either of you touched anything?"

"I heard her scream and I ran across to help…I tried to—to take her pulse," he said, in a voice heavy with shock. "I touched her neck, there."

He pointed a shaky finger at the spot.

"I think I touched the knife handle—but only for a second before I remembered I wasn't supposed to," Rosie said miserably. "I wasn't sure if I should pull it out."

Ryan barely held back a sigh. At times like these, well-intentioned bystanders were often the least helpful people around.

"I need you to step away from Carole's body now," he said, keeping his instructions short and to the point. First responders often succumbed to shock within the first thirty minutes of having witnessed a dead body, and that applied to trained professionals, not just 'have a go heroes'.

"I—yes," Sage mumbled.

Ryan watched him rise on trembling knees, where he stood suspended in the snow, unable to tear his eyes away from the spectacle before him.

That, too, was very common.

"Alright, Marcus, you see the tracks I've made? I want you to follow them back to the castle, where I want you to give either DI MacKenzie, or DS Phillips, your best recollection of what happened here. Can you do that?"

"Yes, I can do that."

"Rosie? I'd like you to follow Marcus and do the same, please."

She rose and began to stumble back towards the castle.

"Chief Inspector?" she said, as something struck her.

Ryan waited.

"When we ran out here, there was only one set of footprints in the snow. I'm sure of it."

So am I, Ryan thought.

"Let's worry about that later," he said, and waited until they'd reached the kitchen door, where MacKenzie and Phillips were waiting to begin the formalities, before turning back to the broken shell of what had once been a woman.

"Definitely not a mini-break," he muttered, and got down to work.

* * *

Though it was plainly unnecessary, Ryan checked Carole's pulse, which confirmed what his eyes had already told him.

The woman was dead.

Not *long* dead, he amended, sliding a hand down the back of her neck to feel the skin, which was still warm to the touch beneath the layers she wore.

The cause of death took very little imagination, since a large, black-handled knife protruded from her gullet. Blood continued to trickle from the edge of the wound, but no longer pumped out onto the snow, as it had done when the wound was first inflicted, judging by the congealing red mass gathered beside her head.

Stepping back, Ryan took out his phone and began to photograph the scene. It was a grisly task but, in the absence of a forensic team, he was left with little choice.

"Need some help, lad?"

The snow crunched beneath Phillips' feet as he made his way over the tracks Ryan had created, stopping a few safe metres short of the body, albeit near enough to see the damage.

"Poor woman," he muttered. "Who'd do this to her?"

Ryan merely shook his head.

"She can't have been dead more than ten minutes," he said. "It only took us a minute to make our way out here, and I assume it was her scream we all heard from the dining room. Her skin is still warm, and the blood on the snow is fresh."

"MacKenzie's taking statements from Marcus and Rosie," Phillips told him. "Anna's helping with crowd management, Dodds is looking out some tarpaulin or rubber sheeting, and I've enlisted David Enfield's help keeping Carole's husband back. He's frantic—ranting and raving about there being a big mistake."

Ryan frowned. "Mistake? That's an odd word to use."

"People say all kinds of odd things, when they've just found out their wife's been murdered."

Ryan inclined his head. "Our priority is to preserve the scene as much as possible," he said, and cast a dubious eye up at the gathering clouds. They'd enjoyed a brief respite, but now it seemed they were in for a second round of bad weather in the not-too-distant future. "I'm going to finish photographing everything and I'll take a video, but then we'll need to move the body. We can't risk any interference from the animals."

Phillips' nose wrinkled, though he knew from long experience it was only the truth.

"There's bound to be something we can use as a stretcher," he said. "Question is, where do we put her?"

The question remained hanging on the air, because, just then, they saw Samuel Black break free of David Enfield's grasp and begin a loping run across the lawn.

Ryan swore, and took off quickly to head him off. He held out his arms in a signal to stop, which Black ignored, and Ryan was forced to perform a muted rugby tackle to keep him from charging forward.

"Woah there! Calm down!"

Samuel twisted this way and that, then gave up the fight and went limp in Ryan's arms.

"They said she was dead," he said. "She can't be. There's been a mistake."

There was that word again, Ryan thought.

"Your wife has been stabbed and has lost her life," he said. "I'm very sorry for your loss."

The words always sounded trite, but it didn't make them any less true.

"No, Chief Inspector. *No.* You don't understand. It was supposed to be a joke. We always take it in turns to play dead on the first morning of an overnight stay—the guests love it, once they get over the shock. So, you see, she can't be dead. She's just pretending."

Ryan filed away the information for later, but shook his head.

"I'm sorry, Mr Black. There's no mistake."

Ordinarily, he would never have advised a relation to view their loved one *in situ*—there were some things that could never be unseen.

But the man was adamant.

"Come with me," Ryan said. "Tread where I tread, and— Samuel?—I want you to remember to breathe and know that I'll be standing there, right beside you."

Black swallowed, then gave a brief, somewhat defiant nod.

"It's all one big joke. You'll see, she's having us all on."

CHAPTER 10

B ut, of course, it was not a joke.

Samuel Black let out a long, keening wail that echoed around the snowy garden and bounced off the castle walls, where the other guests stood watching from the windows of the Great Hall. They saw the butler reach out to his wife, only to be stayed by Ryan's gentle hand on his shoulder.

"I'm sorry, Samuel. It's important you don't touch her, just yet."

"You're—you're sure she's…"

But he could see she was gone, and a single tear leaked down his face.

"Carole," he whispered. "I don't know how this happened. Why—?"

"We're going to find out," Ryan told him, with quiet conviction, and when Samuel looked into his eyes, he could see that he meant it.

This was their stock in trade; what they did every day. For a person to kill right under their noses, to take a life so brazenly despite there being not one, but *three* murder detectives staying under the same roof, demonstrated arrogance of a kind they had rarely encountered.

But Ryan could not discount the possibility of suicide, either.

"Frank, would you take Mr Black back inside the castle and stay with him? I'll finish doing what I can here, and follow you in a moment."

Phillips put a supportive arm around the butler's waist and led him back across the snow and away from what was left of his wife.

"Howay, let's get you inside."

Ryan waited until they were halfway back across the lawn before picking up his task, videoing the area and taking pictures from every angle as he'd seen his friend Tom Faulkner—who was the Senior CSI attached to Northumbria CID—do many times before.

As he was photographing a particularly clear footprint leading towards the body, he caught sight of Dodds rounding the corner of the castle dragging what appeared to be an old-style sledge behind him.

"Will this do?" Dodds asked, holding up a waterproof sheet they used to protect the mattresses. "There's canvas sheeting in the garage, but I can't get the doors open for the snow."

"Don't worry, this is ideal," Ryan said, but frowned at the sledge.

"I thought we could use it to transfer the body," the Estate Manager explained. "I'm afraid we don't have a stretcher."

"Why would you?" Ryan murmured. "Nobody expects to need one."

Dodds nodded.

"There's—ah, there's a storage room, near the North-West tower. We could use that, for now. At least it'll be cold…"

Ryan nodded. The situation was far from ideal, but needs must.

"What happened here, Chief Inspector?" Dodds said quietly. "Was it an accident?"

Ryan looked at the tall, ashen-faced man with a measure of sympathy. Bill Dodds might have shot pheasants or deer and prepared the meat, but there were different kinds of death, and he had no experience with the sort of brutality they were dealing with, now.

"I don't know, yet. But I promise you, I'm going to find out."

* * *

In the end, the sledge proved to be an inspired means of transportation.

Ignoring the small audience watching them from the windows of the Great Hall, Ryan drew on a pair of latex gloves he'd found in a kitchen drawer and carefully removed the knife from Carole's throat, transferring it quickly into a plastic sandwich bag he'd also managed to forage. It was an unenviable task, and served to remind him why he'd chosen not to follow a career in forensic science— or medicine, for that matter. He might have developed a certain resilience in the presence of blood and gore, but this was the first time he'd been called upon to remove a murder weapon and he didn't relish the task.

Dodds, who had wisely looked away while the deed was done, found himself wishing he'd looked away for longer as his stomach performed an uncomfortable somersault at the sight of the gaping wound in the neck of a woman he'd once called his friend. Ryan could be grateful, at least, that there was no spatter as the knife was removed—once the heart stopped beating, the blood stopped pumping around a person's veins and arteries.

"If you need to take a minute, that's understandable," he said to Dodds. "But, if you're going to be sick, do it away from the body, please."

Ryan's prosaic request had the intended effect of pulling him back from the brink, and Dodds sucked in a couple of deep, steadying breaths.

"I'm alright," he said. "I'm okay."

"Good, because I'll need your help rolling her onto this waterproof sheet, in a minute."

Dodds' stomach rolled again.

Ryan finished securing a couple of clear food bags over Carole's hands, using some elastic bands from the Estate Office, and then looked up.

"Ready?"

"As I'll ever be," Dodds mumbled, pulling on his own pair of latex gloves.

"On three," Ryan said, once they had positioned the sheet on the snow nearby and grasped the underside of Carole's stiffening body. "One, two, *three*—"

They wrapped her body in the plastic sheet, cocooning her from prying eyes, then transferred it carefully onto the sledge. They proceeded to tug it across the snow, pausing to lift it through the inner courtyard and on to the storage room near the main entrance. The load was a heavy one, and both men were sweating by the time the grisly task was complete.

"I hope I never have to do that again," Dodds muttered.

Ryan locked the storage room behind them, and pocketed the key.

"I need to make a call," he said, moving on to the next urgent task on his agenda. "Can I use the telephone in the Estate Office?"

Dodds shook his head.

"The outside line went down during the night," he said. "It's only the internal phone network that's working, now. It's a bit of a black hole around here for mobile signal, but you might be able to get a couple of bars if you head into Chatton."

"How far away is Chatton?"

"Couple of miles," the Estate Manager said. "It's the next village over from Chillingham. I'd give you a lift, but the quad bikes are stuck inside the garage. I can try to dig a path, but I'll have to clear off the main gates, too, and that'll take a few hours at the very least."

Ryan thought quickly.

"Is there another gate, or a means of getting across the wall? I'll hike, if I have to, but I need to make that phone call."

Dodds ran a hand over his wiry grey hair, then shrugged.

"There's a smaller side gate that might be a bit easier to clear. I can make a start, if you want?"

Ryan nodded.

"I need to take a statement from you but, as soon as that's done, it would be helpful if you could."

If Dodds was taken aback by the need to give a police statement, he said nothing of it, and simply nodded. He headed off to join the others in the Great Hall, but, rather than going there directly himself, Ryan took a long detour and walked around the outer perimeter of the castle. He found that Dodds had been right when he'd said the snow drifts were as high as his waist; against the west wall of the castle, it had piled even higher. He saw the tracks Dodds had made when he'd been out first thing that morning, and his more recent tracks leading to various outhouses as he'd searched for canvas sheeting.

There were no other tracks in the snow, and none that led directly to where Carole Black had lain, which begged the question of how her killer had managed to get across the snow without leaving a single footprint.

Unless…

Unless, there were ghosts at Chillingham, after all.

CHAPTER 11

When Ryan entered the Great Hall, he found most of the other guests huddled around the fireplace engaged in subdued conversation, trying to make sense of what had happened. Anna was seated beside them, listening quietly, but stood up and crossed the room when she saw Ryan. He wore a shuttered expression that marred his handsome face, one she recognised instantly as being the mask he wore to deal with occasions such as these. In his line of work, there was no room for tears or self-indulgence; his own emotions were shoved mercilessly aside so that he could give his full attention to the job in hand.

Namely, catching a killer.

"Denise is taking a statement from Rosie Baker, in the study," she explained. "Frank's taken Samuel Black to his own apartment—he thought he'd be more comfortable there, away from the crowd."

Ryan nodded, and knew that Phillips could always be relied upon to think of others.

"Where's Marcus?"

"He's gone back to his room, as well. I think he was feeling a bit unwell, after seeing the body."

"Okay. I'll head along and speak to Samuel first, if you're happy to stay here and keep an eye on things?"

She looked back over her shoulder to where the Enfields, the Bakers, Bill Dodds and Nadia Halliwell were seated, trying to give the impression they weren't listening to every word that was being said.

"Don't worry about me," she said. "I've seen enough of your investigations to know how it works. Go and do what you need to do."

He couldn't say why her words affected him so deeply; he only knew that her acceptance and innate understanding that this was the work he was born to do, meant all the world to him.

"Thank you," he said softly, and drew her in for a lingering kiss, uncaring of who might see.

"When will the cavalry be arriving?" she asked, before he moved off in search of the grieving husband. "Did you manage to get through to the Control Room?"

His jaw tightened, the only outward display of anxiety he was likely to show.

"The phone lines are down," he said, under his breath. "I don't want that to be common knowledge, unless somebody asks a direct question. Let's not start a panic."

Anna nodded.

"Bill says we're running out of oil for the boiler tanks, too. They were due to have a delivery this morning, but the tanker couldn't get through. He's going to stoke up the fires and preserve the oil."

Ryan looked out of the picture windows and out across the frozen landscape. Only an hour ago, he'd thought of how pretty it looked; now, he thought of how desolate.

"Chief Inspector!"

The shrill cry came from Sheila Enfield, who rose from her seat and hurried across the room, uncaring that she might be interrupting a private conversation.

"Mrs Enfield."

The woman's short bob of blonde hair had fallen victim to her restless fingers, and was sticking up at interesting angles, a fact which did little to reduce the overall impression of a woman veering dangerously close to the edge.

"It's dreadful," she wailed. "I was saying to David—I was saying, I can't stay here another minute, knowing what's happened to poor Mrs Black. *Such* a lovely woman. If that ghost— whatshername—*Elizabeth,* has struck her down, I don't want to hang around and be next on the list—"

The words came out in one long, high-pitched stream of consciousness, causing both Ryan and Anna to flinch.

"Mrs Enfield, there's no need to panic," he said. "We have everything in hand."

"How can you hope to catch a ghost?" she asked.

Ryan smiled, and made sure his voice carried across the room.

"It wasn't a ghost that killed Carole Black, it was a person— and they're only flesh and blood."

* * *

The Blacks' apartment was located in the eastern wing of the castle, overlooking the inner courtyard. It was a cosy space, sheltered from the worst of the wind and snow, and filled with chintzy cushions and porcelain ornaments of the kind Ryan's mother liked to collect. Where the rest of the castle was a trove of historic treasures, here was a more modern space where the working couple had lived. Ryan could imagine them coming here at the end of a long day, exchanging stories about the guests who happened to be visiting and occasionally bickering, as all couples did.

Now, only one of them survived, and his gaunt figure was slumped in one of the overstuffed armchairs his wife had arranged around a coffee table. Phillips had made him a cup of tea, which stood on a coaster untouched and was now developing a milky skin as Samuel Black stared vacantly at the wall.

"He's hardly moved from that spot," Phillips murmured. "I've tried giving him a biscuit, to keep his blood sugar up, but he's having none of it."

"A bit of shock, you think?"

Phillips nodded.

"When's Morrison sending a team over?" he asked.

"She isn't," Ryan said bluntly. "The lines are down, so I haven't been able to call her, or anyone else, for that matter."

Frank Phillips prided himself on being able to hold his own in most situations, and didn't consider himself the kind of man who was easily spooked—not counting altercations with wild cattle, of course. Yet, now, he felt a flicker of fear.

"What're we going to do?" he wondered.

"The driveway's impassable," Ryan said. "It'll take a day to clear the snow from around the gates, and that's not counting the rest of the driveway, or the roads beyond. Until somebody gets a snowplough up here, or the snow starts to melt, we're stuck."

Phillips swallowed.

"Not to be all doom and gloom, but I don't much fancy being stuck in a castle with a raving lunatic roaming around."

"Words to live by," Ryan agreed. "Which is why I'm declaring extraordinary measures, Frank. We approach this like any other investigation, but we stay vigilant at all times. There's a dungeon full of weaponry for the taking, if a person was so inclined. Let's keep things as calm and as quiet as possible, so nobody starts to panic."

"The guests, you mean?"

"No," Ryan muttered. "Carole's killer."

CHAPTER 12

In the space of a couple of hours, Samuel Black looked as though he'd aged ten years. His skin was an unnatural shade of grey, and he seemed to be mumbling to himself as he stared at a framed print of Van Gogh's *Sunflowers* on the wall.

"How are you holding up, Samuel?"

The butler turned to Ryan with an air of distraction.

"Sorry?"

"I asked how you're holding up," Ryan repeated gently, and set his mobile phone to record their discussion. "I want to say again how very sorry we all are for your loss. I have no current means of contacting my colleagues at Northumbria CID, but I'll be making every effort to speak to them before the day is over, so we can work together to find the truth."

"Carole used to say I'd have made a good policeman," Samuel said, conversationally. "She said she liked the uniform."

Ryan and Phillips exchanged a glance.

"Well, bearing that in mind, perhaps you could help us investigate what happened here, today," Ryan said, keeping a sharp eye on the older man. "If it's alright with you, I'm going to record our conversation in case we need any of the information you tell me further down the line. Okay?"

Samuel nodded, and Ryan reeled off the names of those present, their badge numbers, and the date, time and location of the interview. He also checked Samuel's identification before proceeding.

"How long had you and Carole been married, Samuel?"

"Twenty-two years," he replied, without needing to think about it. "We went to South America for our twentieth wedding anniversary a couple of years ago. Carole always wanted to go to Buenos Aires, after she'd seen *Evita* at the theatre."

Ryan nodded.

"How long have you worked at the castle?"

"About sixteen years," he replied. "A position came up for a butler-valet, and we'd always loved Northumberland. Carole planned to find work outside the castle, but the housekeeper was due to retire, and she was offered the position once it became vacant. It was serendipitous, really, because—"

He broke off, suddenly.

"You don't need to know about all that."

"Any information you can give me is useful," Ryan said. "What were you going to say?"

"It's all water under the bridge, but we're both lucky to have found well-paying jobs that we enjoy," Samuel said. "A few years ago, we lost our savings on some risky investments, and it set us back a bit. It's been a relief for both of us to be able to keep working, and we've been trying to build up a little nest egg to replace the one we lost."

Ryan nodded again.

"Was Carole happy, too?" he asked, carefully.

There was a tiny pause, and then Samuel nodded.

"I think so. She likes anything to do with the occult, and Chillingham's the perfect place to go ghost hunting."

"And you?" Ryan asked. "Are you interested in that side of things?"

Samuel pressed his lips together, unwilling to be disloyal and yet too honourable to lie.

"Carole was interested enough for the both of us," he replied. "That's why—that's why I agreed to go along with all the silly tricks she liked to play on the guests—"

"You mean, like the one she was planning to play this morning?"

Tears filled Samuel's eyes, and he nodded.

"Why don't you talk us through your movements?" Ryan suggested, to keep the man focused just a little while longer.

Black pinched the bridge of his nose.

"I woke up about five-thirty," he said. "Carole usually wakes up ten or fifteen minutes after I do, at around quarter-to-six. We both needed to be up early, to make a start on serving breakfast from seven."

"I see. And then?"

It was imperative that he was armed with as many facts as possible, while they remained fresh in the man's mind but, in Ryan's experience, a victim's family tended to shut down after about twenty minutes, at best. It was his job to extract as much useful information as possible, without compromising on compassion.

It was a delicate balance to strike.

"Ah, well, I made sure I was in the dining room at ten-to-seven. Breakfast is served from seven until ten-thirty, at weekends," he explained.

"Who was the first guest to arrive for breakfast?" Ryan asked.

"That was the Bakers. They arrived bang on seven o'clock."

"How did they seem to you? Were they in good spirits?"

Samuel spent his days answering the wants and whims of those he served; there was no better person to speak to about reading human behaviour than a man who spent all day observing it.

"I'd have said they were both less animated than when they arrived yesterday," Samuel replied. "I assumed that to be because of what happened at the séance last night, although neither of them said as much."

"What time did they leave the dining room?"

Samuel frowned as he cast his mind back.

"I'd have said around an hour later, at about eight-thirty. They took their time over eggs and bacon, and exchanged a friendly word with the Enfields, who came in at around quarter past eight. I believe your party arrived at around quarter-to-nine, shortly before Bill Dodds and Miss Halliwell."

"Well remembered," Ryan murmured.

"I have an eye for these things," Samuel admitted. "But, in this case, I was also looking to see who would be there at nine o'clock."

Something clicked neatly into place in Ryan's mind. Seconds before he'd heard a scream, they'd heard the chiming of the castle bell sounding the hour, a small fact he'd managed to overlook until then.

"Tell me about this game your wife concocted," Ryan said.

"We host a number of weekend ghost tours during the year," Samuel explained. "Some are one-night stays, some are two, but Carole liked to make sure people got their money's worth, I suppose. Usually, she would dress up in old Victorian garb and stage a death, or run through the corridor at night with a torch or a lantern. It made her laugh, so I went along with it," he said, and sighed deeply. "This time, Carole thought it would be a good idea to stage a 'floating ghost murder'. There's a legend, you see, about a lady of the house having been found lying on the south lawn hundreds of years ago, having been stabbed—"

Samuel trailed off, as an image of Carole lying in the snow with a knife in her throat resurfaced. He saw her eyes staring up at him all over again, and remembered how full of sparkle they'd once been.

"I—I—"

"Take your time," Phillips said, and put a steadying hand on the man's shoulder. "Nearly done, now."

Samuel nodded, wiping a thin layer of sweat from his brow.

"The idea was that Carole would sneak out of the kitchen and be ready to scream at nine o'clock," he managed. "That's the time when the breakfast room is usually at its busiest, so there was less chance people would be wandering around to catch her heading out onto the lawn."

"Did she plan to take a knife with her?" Ryan asked.

Samuel shook his head.

"Not that I know of," he said, thinking back to the black obsidian letter knife plunged into his wife's throat, all the way to the hilt. "But that knife is part of the castle's collection. It normally lives on the writing table in the study adjoining the Great Hall. Anybody could have picked it up."

Ryan agreed.

"Did you discuss the plan in here, or with anyone else?"

"I—well, I suppose we chatted about it in the kitchen this morning, and she might have mentioned it sometime yesterday, but I can't really remember…"

Ryan saw the man's eyes starting to droop as emotional fatigue set in, and knew his time was almost up.

"One last question, Samuel, then we'll leave you to rest. Do you know of any reason why Carole would have wanted to fall on the knife herself?"

Samuel shook his head.

"She was the strongest person I knew," he said softly. "Much stronger than me. We've had our ups and downs, but nothing's ever broken her, and nothing ever would. If she's dead, it's because somebody killed her."

"Do you know of any enemies she might have had, or anyone with a reason to kill?"

Samuel glanced across at him, then away again.

"No. Nobody."

Ryan frowned, but didn't press the matter.

"Thank you, Mr Black. We appreciate all your help at this very difficult time. With your permission, we'd like to take a look at your wife's things?"

Samuel lifted a shoulder.

"Look at whatever you like," he said. "She isn't here to argue."

With a final word of condolence, they went off to conduct a fingertip search of Carole's belongings, leaving her husband to his memories.

CHAPTER 13

B y the time Ryan and Phillips had finished interviewing Samuel Black, MacKenzie had also completed her interview with Rosie Baker, and had escorted her back to the Great Hall.

"How'd you find her?" Ryan asked, as Rosie was reunited with her mother, who proceeded to fuss over her as though she was a teenager and not a woman of twenty-seven.

"Emotional," MacKenzie replied, succinctly. "But quite clear, once we got down to the bones of it. She says she and her mother were up with the larks—apparently, they couldn't sleep after that séance—and went to breakfast on the dot of seven. They were the first ones there, so she tells me."

"That tallies with what Samuel Black's just told us," Phillips said.

She nodded.

"Rosie says her mum wasn't feeling well, after breakfast, so she went back to their apartment for a lie down while she explored some of the ground floor. She heard the scream as she was about to go up the stairs to the Great Hall, but ended up running back out through the doors to the south lawn, instead."

"Did she run into Marcus Sage?"

"She says he'd beaten her to it, and had just reached Carole's body by the time she stepped outside. She ran across to join him, which couldn't have taken more than thirty seconds, maybe forty-five at a push."

"It only takes ten," Ryan said. "Perhaps it's time to interview Mr Sage?"

"You two do the honours," Phillips said. "I'll keep Anna company in here."

* * *

Marcus Sage and Nadia Halliwell were staying in the finest guest apartment available, known as the 'Grey Apartment' and named after the family who had ruled over Chillingham Castle from the thirteenth century to the 1980s. As they made their way towards it, MacKenzie's mind boggled at the idea of being able to trace her family lineage so far back, being fairly certain that her own genealogy consisted of a long line of arable farmers in County Kerry, of which she was rightly proud.

All the same, she wondered what it would be like to grow up in a castle, or to have entertained kings and queens.

"How the other half live, eh?" she joked, as they passed along a plush corridor filled with *objets d'art*. "Is this what your dad's place is like, down in Devon?"

Ryan pulled a face, never having felt comfortable in such surroundings, always having wished for a more 'normal' life. His father was a former high-ranking diplomat, a fact he seldom discussed outside of his closest circle, for security reasons apart from anything else. But there was another reason, too, and that had much more to do with social inequality.

"It's easy for me to talk about the excesses of the rich, or the imbalance between the wealthy and the poor in this country," he said. "But it sounds hypocritical, even to my own ears. Who am I to complain, since I benefited from my family's position, had the best of everything and a top-class education? But, for what it's worth, I plan to give away most of my inheritance."

MacKenzie stopped dead in the corridor and turned to him. There was important work to be done, but friendship came first.

"That was a thoughtless joke I made, and I'm sorry," she said. "The fact is, I forget—we all forget—about where you've come from, because you don't wear it on your sleeve. You don't swan around flashing the cash, and you don't talk with marbles in your mouth."

She gave him a lopsided smile.

"You treat everyone the same, Ryan, and you've never made any of us feel small or inferior in any way—"

"You don't have to—"

She held up a hand for silence, having recently developed her own maternal powers whilst parenting Samantha. Ryan might only have been a handful of years her junior but, at times like these, she felt protective.

"Let me finish," she said. "You're one of the most fair-minded people I know, which is why you're not only my boss, you're my friend—and Frank's too. You believe in the things that matter, the things that matter *here*," she said, patting a hand to her heart. "That matters more than where you were born, or to whom. You shouldn't be asked to apologise for having been born wealthy, Ryan. The point is, you have a kind family, who've clearly taught you the right values. You don't need to tell me you're giving it all away, as soon as you can; it doesn't surprise me at all that you'd want to share what you have. It's who you are."

Ryan was embarrassed to feel his throat burning, and he took a couple of seconds to recover himself before replying.

"Thank you, Denise. Your friendship, and Frank's, is one of the most important things I could ever hope to have."

A bit overcome herself, she leaned in to press a kiss against his cheek.

"Right, let's get back to work," she said briskly. "This case isn't going to solve itself."

"Yes, ma'am," he grinned.

* * *

When Marcus Sage answered the door, he looked distinctly worse for wear.

"I suppose you're here to take a statement?"

At Ryan's affirmative, he gestured them inside the apartment and led them into the sitting room.

"Seeing the body earlier got to me a bit, I'm afraid. I've been chained to the toilet bowl ever since we came back inside," he said.

"Sorry to hear that, Mr Sage," MacKenzie said. "Can we get you some water?"

He shook his head.

"In that case, we'd like to take down your statement concerning the sad events of this morning," she continued. "Do you have any form of identification to hand?"

He raised an eyebrow.

"What do you need to see my ID for? I'm not drinking underage."

"It's procedure," she said, with a smile. "As part of our investigations, we're required to confirm your age and identity."

He shrugged, and pulled out his driver's license, which Ryan photographed on his phone.

"Thank you," he said, handing it back. "Now, Mr Sage—"

"Marcus."

"Marcus," Ryan repeated. "I'm going to need to record this interview, which has been the same for everyone we've interviewed so far."

Receiving no complaints, he set his phone to 'record' and proceeded with the formalities.

"Now, Marcus, why don't you start by telling us a bit about yourself. I see from your licence that you're thirty-nine, and that you live in Durham. That's a nice part of the world…what line of work are you in?"

"Property development."

Ryan nodded.

"How long have you been doing that?"

"Sorry—what does this have to do with what happened this morning?" Sage interjected.

"Just trying to build up a picture," MacKenzie told him. "Have you always been in the business of property development?"

Marcus licked his lips and rose to pour himself a glass of water.

"I was in sales, before that," he said, after a couple of gulps.

"I see," Ryan said. "And how did you meet Miss Halliwell?"

Marcus heaved a sigh and gestured with his glass, as if the topic bored him.

"On the scene…you know."

Ryan and MacKenzie's faces remained blank.

"The scene?"

"I'm part-owner of a couple of clubs, a few wine bars. I go out most Fridays and Saturdays to socialise. You tend to see the same faces after a while, the same girls…" He drained the rest of his glass and set it back down. "I saw Nadia around a few times, we had a few laughs, and now I can't get rid of her."

If his last comment was intended to be a joke, it fell like a lead balloon.

"How long have you and Miss Halliwell been seeing one another?" Ryan asked.

"I dunno," Marcus said. "Two months, maybe three? You'd be better off asking her."

"And whose idea was it to come here, to Chillingham?"

"Hers, of course. She said she'd won a weekend in the country, all expenses paid, and promised to make it a dirty one—"

He sent MacKenzie what passed for an apologetic smile.

"Sorry, love, but you know how men think."

"Do I?" she murmured. "And that's Detective Inspector MacKenzie, if you don't mind."

Sage's face fell into a sneer, and she experienced the same sensation of unease she'd felt the night before, sitting beside him at the banqueting table. Her skin began to prickle, and adrenaline leaked into her system, preparing her for fight or flight.

Suddenly, she remembered where she'd felt something similar before.

Keir Edwards.

The Hacker.

CHAPTER 14

Though Marcus Sage was not the serial killer known to many as 'The Hacker', MacKenzie experienced a visceral response similar to the one she'd lived through during her time in captivity. It had been three years since that dark time, and most days she managed to forget.

But not today.

Sage's demeanour, his expensive clothes and the cold, dead look in his eye, all reminded her of the man she'd survived, and she had to ask herself whether she was able to do her job objectively. They had no evidence to suggest this man was in any way guilty—not of Carole's murder or any other crime—and she was always the first to say that instinct should not be relied upon over hard facts.

"Had you ever met Mrs Black, prior to coming here?" Ryan asked.

Sage shook his head.

"Never. I don't think we move in the same circles, do you?"

Ryan ignored that.

"Moving on to the events earlier this morning, would you mind telling us your movements?"

Sage blew out a gusty breath.

"We woke up around eight, thanks to the castle clock," he said. "Nadia needed a coffee, so she had a shower before me and headed off to breakfast around half past, or something like that. I didn't check the time. I needed the gents, so I popped in there on the way—"

"Around what time?" MacKenzie asked.

"Must've been just before nine," he said. "Anyway, I used the loo and was about to head back upstairs when I heard the scream."

"What did you do?"

"I had a look through the window and saw somebody lying in the snow, so I did what anyone would do. I ran outside to see if she needed help."

"How could you tell it was a 'she'?" Ryan wondered.

"It was the puffa jacket," Sage replied. "I recognised it as being Carole's."

"And, did you see anyone else, acting suspiciously?"

He sat down again and shook his head.

"I wish I had," he said. "It'd make things a lot easier, wouldn't it?"

"How so?"

"Well, I know you must be thinking it was me who killed her," Sage replied, without batting an eyelid. "I would, if I were you."

"Really? Why would we think that, Mr Sage?"

"Well, it stands to reason, doesn't it?" he replied. "I could only see one set of footprints when I ran out there, which looks pretty bad for me, unless she committed suicide using that bloody great knife."

Ryan and MacKenzie said nothing.

"Look, all I can tell you is that the woman was already dead when I found her," Sage continued. "I checked her pulse, but it was pretty obvious she was gone. A few seconds later, I spotted that lass—Rosie Barker, or Baker, or whatever she's called—running out as well."

He leaned back against the sofa.

"You know the rest."

Ryan leaned forward in his chair and rested his forearms on his knees, to create an air of confidence that often worked with skittish witnesses.

"Tell me, Marcus, how do you think she died?"

Sage looked surprised, but raised his arms above his head to link his fingers behind his ears in a relaxed pose as he gave the question some thought.

"Well, it has to be suicide," he said, eventually. "There's no other explanation for it. She must've fallen on the knife, or something."

"It seems an unusual place to commit suicide," Ryan mused.

"I dunno, she was telling us all about some ancestor or other who went out there a couple of hundred years ago and killed herself…you know she was into all those ghosts and ghoulies. Maybe it all went to her head, a bit."

"Well," MacKenzie said. "We'll certainly bear that theory in mind. In the meantime, I wonder if you'd be so good as to lend us your fingerprints, for the purposes of the investigation?"

"I don't—"

"It's perfectly normal procedure," Ryan assured him, while MacKenzie reached for the ink bottle and paper she'd spotted on the desk nearby.

"Don't you coppers have a better way of doing this?" he asked, as the blue ink stained his skin.

"Sometimes, the old-fashioned methods are the best," Ryan replied, and pressed his thumb down hard on a piece of notepaper.

* * *

As the door shut behind them, MacKenzie let out the breath she'd been holding in her chest.

"Everything alright?" Ryan asked. "You turned a bit pale, back there."

"There's just something about him," she said. "I don't know what it is; he's a misogynist, but it usually takes more than that to get my hackles up."

She paused, wondering whether to bring it up, given Ryan's own personal hatred of The Hacker, but decided honesty was the best policy.

"To tell you the truth, he reminded me a bit of Keir Edwards," she said.

"Me too," he surprised her by saying. "What? You didn't think I'd notice the similarities? The man's a raging narcissist, he's controlling, and he's evasive. I don't need access to the police database to know he's probably got a sheet, but having a few misdemeanours doesn't make him a killer."

"That we know of," MacKenzie murmured.

"It's a constant challenge, battling the memories you and I both carry of men like Keir Edwards," he said. "They're intrusive, and come back at the most inopportune moments."

"Like at bedtime," she smiled.

"Exactly. But we're good at our jobs, Denise. We know when we're skating the line, and when we're pushing because we have to. And, with that one in there? Believe me, we have to push, but not too hard until we're sure, and not until we've got the right support."

MacKenzie wrapped her arms around herself, feeling a wintry chill snake up and down her spine, like fingers.

"There's four of us, and only one of them, whoever it may be," she said. "If it came to it, we can overpower them."

"You and I both know how quickly someone like that can strike," he replied. "Carole Black was only out there in the snow for a couple of minutes, before somebody silenced her."

"Silenced her?"

"Of course," Ryan said. "The knife in the gullet wasn't just expedient; I think it was *symbolic*. We need to find out why."

"Because of what she said last night, at the séance? Or at another time?"

Ryan's lips twisted.

"Could be either, or both. I've got a boxful of Carole's belongings to start sifting through, but I'm betting anything interesting is under lock and key somewhere. She had a whole set of keys in her pocket when she died, and I want to find out where they each lead, starting with the filing cabinets in the Estate Office."

"You reckon she was blackmailing someone?"

Ryan stuck his hands in his pockets, loathe to speak ill of the dead, even when their actions hadn't been laudable while they were living.

"Earlier, Samuel told us they'd struggled financially for a while, after some risky investment scheme that didn't pay off. Working here is fine, but did you see the watch Carole wore? The jewellery?

That doesn't come cheap, especially not for a couple who're supposed to be rebuilding. If I had access to her bank accounts, I'd be looking for small, regular cash deposits, or one-off larger ones—unless she stashed some cash around the castle."

"We need reinforcements," she said.

"I'm going to walk into Chatton and find a telephone or some mobile signal—whichever comes first."

MacKenzie frowned. "It'll be dark in a couple of hours, and it'll take you that long to get there, through all that snow. Are you sure it's a good idea?"

"We don't have a choice," Ryan said. "If we wait until the snow clears, whoever killed that woman will be out of here like a bat out of hell, and there'd be nothing we could do to stop them."

"There's a dungeon," she reminded him. "Let's not rule it out, too soon."

CHAPTER 15

When they returned to the Great Hall, there was mutiny afoot.

"If you think for one *second* that I'm going to stay trapped in this castle with a—a *murderer,* then you've got another thing coming!"

Sheila Enfield's voice rose to a dangerously high octave, as she jabbed a long, sparkly manicured finger at Phillips' chest.

"Aye, and that goes for me, too," her husband said. "If there's some maniac on the loose, the last thing I want to do is wait around like a sitting duck—"

"Now, you need to just *keep calm,*" Phillips said. "For one thing, we haven't ruled out accidental death, yet. For another, nobody's trapped here—"

"How the heck d'you explain how Carole Black managed to get all the way across the lawn and stab herself, then?" Sheila raged.

"Well, she could have fallen on the knife," Phillips said, reasonably. "As I say, nothing has been ruled out, just yet—"

"And, as for not feeling trapped, have you taken a look outside? I can't even see the driveway, and the front doors won't open, only the back. Our cars are all snowed in, and Bill says that the main gates are completely snowed under. How am I supposed to get out of here, unless you expect me to sprout wings and *fly?*"

"Now, listen here, there's no cause to be rude," Phillips said, and his voice held a warning. He might be a good, kind-hearted man, but he'd grown up on the streets that he now policed, and *had* never, nor *would* ever, accept any nonsense.

"Is it true that the phone lines are down?" Nadia chimed in, wringing her hands. "Does that mean we can't even call for help?"

Amid the rising wave of panic, Ryan judged it the opportune moment to step in.

"As my sergeant has already said, we're pursuing all relevant lines of enquiry and haven't ruled out the possibility of an accidental death at this time. As for the roads, how're they looking, Bill?"

The Estate Manager tucked his thumbs into the pockets of his cargo trousers.

"All the farmers in the area will be concerned about stranded livestock," he said. "They'll be looking to clear the roads as soon as possible, as will I, but there's just no chance of it, yet."

"See? *See?* I told you, we're trapped in here—"

"Rather than focusing on your own misfortune, perhaps spare a thought for the man who lost his wife today," Ryan said, deftly taking the wind out of her sails. "Samuel is grieving and won't be available to cook or clean, nor would we expect him to. I suggest that everyone stays inside the castle and try to stay with the group, where it's warm and dry. I'd also suggest we divvy up the jobs for tonight and tomorrow—is anybody willing to cook dinner, whilst others do the washing up?"

Jacqui Baker raised her hand.

"I like to cook," she said, shyly.

Her daughter and Nadia offered to help, whilst David Enfield was shamed into offering his services in the washing up department.

"Good," Ryan said. "If we stick together, we'll come through this. In the meantime, don't go wandering off anywhere alone—"

"What will you be doing?" Sheila demanded.

Ryan looked at her, very coolly.

"Rather than following my own advice, I'll be walking to Chatton, to find a telephone."

"Not on your own, you won't."

Anna stepped forward with a challenging look in her eye.

"If you think I'm letting the future father of my children wander off into the Great Unknown and freeze to death in a snowdrift somewhere, you haven't been paying attention all these years."

He smiled, knowing that to argue would be a waste of time.

"In that case, better get our skates on, while there's still a bit of daylight left."

* * *

While Ryan and Anna bundled themselves into clothing even Arctic explorers would have been proud of, Phillips and MacKenzie made their way back to The Lookout. Eyes and ears seemed to lurk in every shadow, and, more than once, they'd felt as though they were not alone despite there being nobody else there.

"I'm tellin' you," Phillips declared, once they'd collapsed onto the sofa. "The lad's cursed."

"*Cursed?* Don't be ridiculous, Frank."

"Well, how else do you explain the fact that, every blinkin' holiday, without fail, a murder pops up—"

"Frank…"

"First, it was that time on Holy Island," Phillips said, ticking them off his fingers. "He was supposed to be up there resting and recuperating then, lo and behold, a murder…"

"He also happened to meet his future wife on that island," MacKenzie reminded him.

"Purely incidental," he said. "What about that time in Florence? All that pasta, and I hardly got to eat a bite of it, what with all the murders and the mayhem—"

"You *did* get to marry me, while you were out there," she reminded him sternly. "Or did you forget?"

"As if I could," Phillips crooned.

"Hmph."

"What about up at Cragside, when they were staying in the cottage up there? You'd think there'd be no time for anything but enjoying the trees and the birds…but, practically as soon as he sets foot in the place, the lights all go haywire and he's sniffing out all kinds of dark deeds. I'm tellin' you, pet, we should think about hiring an exorcist."

MacKenzie laughed richly.

"Frank, have I told you lately how much I love you?"

"I could stand to hear it again," he said, and gave her a winning smile.

"Well, I do. Despite some of the daft stuff you come out with."

"Well, you'd better strap yourself in, because I'm about to come out with some more," he said, and she rolled her eyes heavenward.

"Come on, then."

"Well, I was just thinking…what if somebody killed Carole using a crossbow?"

"*What?*"

"Well, I mean, they've got all kinds of Mediaeval implements down in the dungeons. What if somebody borrowed one of them and shot her from one of the windows?"

MacKenzie was about to dismiss the idea out of hand, but was forced to admit that it was possible.

A *remote* possibility, but still possible.

"How do you explain the fact that the wound was to the front of Carole's throat?" she asked. "Firstly, they'd have to be an excellent marksman, and, secondly, they'd have been much more likely to shoot her in the back as she walked away from the castle, if they were firing from one of the windows."

Phillips puffed out his cheeks, then let the air out in a frustrated sigh.

"Well, we're back to square one, because I can't see how anybody could float across the snow to kill her, leaving no footprints at all."

"Maybe they didn't have to," she said, cryptically. "Ryan's secured the body and documented the scene as best he can. We've interviewed everybody in the castle and recorded their statements. Ryan bagged the murder weapon and you've both searched the victim's home. That isn't bad going, considering only a few hours ago Carole Black was living and breathing like the rest of us, and we've had no outside help from forensics."

Phillips had to admit his wife had a point.

"There's another possibility I was thinking of," he said.

"Which is?"

"What if Carole was stabbed inside the castle, and then she staggered outside to try to attract attention from all of us who were up in the dining room?"

MacKenzie shook her head.

"The footprints Carole made were straight and uniform…if she'd been staggering or running, they'd have been haphazard."

Phillips folded his arms.

"That's very inconvenient."

"Especially for Carole," MacKenzie agreed.

CHAPTER 16

While Ryan and his team went about the business of investigating murder, Bill Dodds had spent much of the afternoon clearing a pathway through the snow, to enable Ryan to leave the castle and walk to Chatton. It ran from the doors on the south of the castle, skirted around its perimeter and through a couple of narrow gates, past a selection of stone outhouses, through heavy woodland lining the driveway until it reached a small opening in the wall leading out of the castle grounds and into the graveyard of St Peter's church—a tiny, ancient stone edifice just outside the main gates and behind the lodge, where many of the castle's ancestors were buried and, it was said, where their souls continued to haunt those who trespassed on their domain.

Armed with provisions and torches, their bodies wrapped in the thickest clothing they could find, Anna and Ryan stepped out into the cold twilight and prepared to face an unpleasant journey ahead.

"Are you sure you want to do this?" Ryan asked. "I don't want you to get hurt—"

"I could say the same of you," she shot back. "We're both young and fit. We'll survive."

Ryan had to admit that the thought of leaving her in the castle at the mercy of a motley crew of strangers, one of whom he knew to be a cold-blooded killer, held little attraction for him either; even with Phillips and MacKenzie there to help. It only took a second

91

to plunge a knife through flesh and bone, and even the most vigilant friends could not watch over her all the time.

But then, Anna wouldn't thank anybody for clucking around her like a mother hen.

"I know how strong you are," he said, as they began to follow the pathway Dodds had shovelled for them. "It's because I know you've had your fair share of drama in the past that I want to protect you from any more, that's all."

"I know, and I love you for it," she said, reaching out to grasp his hand. "But you can't wrap me in cotton wool and overlook your own safety. You're not invincible."

As if to prove her point, Ryan skidded on a patch of ice and almost lost his footing, but it was she who steadied him.

"Thanks, and, for the record, one thing I know for sure is that I'm not invincible," he said, thinking of the scars his body bore, from all the gunshots and stabbings he'd survived over the years. "Maybe I've got nine lives, like a cat."

"I worry for you, every time you leave for work," she said.

"Try not to," he said, though he knew it was an impossible task. "In any case, some of the students you have to deal with at the university are more terrifying than most of the criminals I face down in the average working week. By rights, it's you I should be worrying about."

She smiled, but it didn't quite reach her eyes.

"I mean it, Ryan. You don't realise how the rest of the world sees you," she said, trying to make him understand. "Some people admire you, for all that you stand for—I'm one of them—but others resent you. They don't want to be reminded of their own shortcomings, or have you interfering with the way they want to live their lives. You're a hero, but you're also a target."

"A *hero?*"

"Yeah, well, don't let it go to your head."

He grew serious again.

"I know you're right," he said, and held out his hand as they reached another slippery patch leading down to the woodland. "There was a time when my own safety didn't matter so much, because it was just me and an empty flat to look forward to. But now, I have you, and a life I want to come home to each night. Believe me, I never take it for granted, and I don't take unnecessary risks."

The sun made its descent into the horizon, sending wide arcs of flaming light bouncing off the shimmering white hills in a final act of glorious defiance. They turned to watch it, marvelling at the sky that was a melting pot of pink and orange.

But, in the east, portentous grey clouds were gathering.

"We'd better hurry," she said. "It looks like another storm's brewing."

* * *

Back at the castle, Phillips and MacKenzie made their way to the Estate Office, which was empty while Bill Dodds joined the others in preparing dinner. They used Carole's keychain to unlock the door, and then flicked on the overhead light to brighten the space, which had taken on an empty, hollow feeling now that one of its regular inhabitants had died.

It was funny how rooms, and houses, could reflect the mood of their occupants.

LJ Ross

"I'll make a start on the desk, if you do the filing cabinets," MacKenzie said, and they began a systematic search of all the locked drawers.

"Do you really think Ryan's on to something, with this blackmail idea?"

"It makes sense," MacKenzie replied. "Carole must have known something and tried to use that knowledge as leverage. Unless another motive comes to light, or we discover it was accidental death, it's the most plausible theory."

"Hopefully, Lowerson or Yates'll be able to help us out with some background searches, once Ryan gets through to the office," Phillips said, referring to the two junior members of their team back at Northumbria CID. Melanie Yates and Jack Lowerson could always be relied upon to sniff out anything nefarious in a person's past.

If Ryan managed to get through to them.

"I hope they're alright out there," he added, glancing out at the last embers of daylight. "They'll be exhausted, by the time they come back."

If they came back.

"They have each other," MacKenzie said, and tried another of the keys on Carole's chain, until she found the one that opened her main desk drawer. "Here we are."

MacKenzie rooted around the drawer, but found nothing except half-used biros, post-it notes and an inordinate number of drawing pins.

"Must have been on special offer," she muttered.

Across the room, Phillips tried all the keys in the filing cabinets until he found the right one, and, when he did, made a small sound of triumph.

They spent a few minutes rifling through the files, before he paused.

"Shouldn't we get a warrant for this?"

"Extraordinary measures, remember?"

"Is that a real thing? I haven't seen it in the guidelines…"

"Frank, when you're trapped in a thirteenth-century castle with a killer, a bunch of ghosts and a dead body locked in the storeroom, you'd better believe 'extraordinary measures' is a real thing. It's every man or woman for himself, and that includes rifling through the odd filing cabinet."

"Well, when you put it like that."

But, after a thorough search, they found nothing untoward.

"Maybe Carole didn't keep records," Phillips replied. "Or, maybe, she didn't die because of something she was doing."

"They always keep records," MacKenzie said. "And people don't usually get stabbed in the throat for no reason."

They locked the Estate Office behind them, and almost jumped out of their skins when the castle clock chimed loudly above their heads.

Four o'clock.

"I asked Ryan to put a call through to Samantha when he gets to Chatton" Phillips said.

"Good thinking. She was fine when I spoke to her yesterday, but I'm starting to worry about her."

Phillips nodded.

"My girl's a tough cookie," he said, drawing her in for a kiss. "They both are."

Her lips curved.

"The fostering agency said we'd hear back from the adoption panel by the first week of January."

He felt the same trickle of fear as he always did, whenever the discussion came up. Almost from the first moment Samantha had come to stay with them, he'd thought of her as his daughter. She'd slotted into their lives like the missing piece of a jigsaw puzzle, and there seemed nothing more natural than making it official. Life without her now was unimaginable, and the prospect of an adoption panel ruling against their application was something he could scarcely bear to think about.

"There's no reason why they shouldn't decide in our favour," he said. "We're both upstanding members of the community, aren't we?"

"Doesn't get more upstanding than a pair of murder detectives," she agreed. "But we're older, Frank. And our work takes us away from home, sometimes."

"Ah, bollocks to that. We're only in our forties and fifties and, besides, you're only as old as you feel *inside,*" he said. "I don't know about you, but I feel about twenty-one."

She looked at the thinning hair on his head and the weathered lines on his face, and couldn't have loved him more.

"I'm not sure these people agree with that kind of logic," she said.

"Well, they'll have to see sense, won't they? As for work…there are thousands of working parents in this country! How do they expect people to earn a living?"

"Even if we could afford to, I'd be so bored staying at home," MacKenzie admitted. "My mother spent her whole life cooking, cleaning and looking after us kids, and there's no shame in it. That's a full-time job in itself, and my father worked another full-time job bringing in the money. But you know what, Frank? I've always wondered if she was capable of more."

He nodded, thinking that his own family had been much the same.

"It was more common, in the old days, for the man to go out to work—"

"Not *that* old, thank you very much."

He chuckled, and then turned to take her in his arms.

"It'll be alright, love. You'll see."

CHAPTER 17

The journey from Chillingham to Chatton was less than two miles, but to Ryan and Anna it might have been five times that distance. With snow piled high on the roads and no friendly tyre tracks to lend a hand, it took the pair much longer to cover the ground, eager as they were to make it to Chatton before nightfall. They knocked on the doors of houses they passed by, in the hope of finding one with a working telephone, but it was as though the village of Chillingham had been abandoned.

"It's creepy, isn't it?" Anna said, as they passed by empty houses, along roads with no footprints or tyre tracks.

"Maybe they're all out of town, visiting relatives," Ryan said, reaching out to hold her hand as the shadows lengthened.

"Maybe," she said, doubtfully. "Ryan, look!"

Anna planted her feet in the snow and tilted her head up to the sky, which was blanketed with stars twinkling in the uppermost heavens. He did the same and they stood there for long minutes—two small, insignificant beings in a vast universe.

"Storms still coming in our direction," Ryan said, pointing to the east, where the stars could no longer be seen.

They headed off again at a brisk pace, their feet crunching against the packed snow.

"Do you think anybody will be able to get up here tomorrow?" she asked. "I mean, even if we find a telephone, do you think anybody will be able to help?"

Ryan had been asking himself the same question.

"Honestly? I don't know. It depends on whether the main road has been reopened."

"At least you'll be able to ask Jack or Melanie to do some checks for you," she said.

"I will, but how will they let me know the outcome? We need to head back to the castle tonight, so they'll have no means of contacting us with the results, if the phone lines don't get back up and running again."

"Do you have any idea who killed Carole?"

Ryan glanced across, but didn't break stride.

"I already know who killed Carole Black. It's just a question of proving it beyond a reasonable doubt."

* * *

Twenty minutes later, they reached the outskirts of Chatton. It was a larger village than the one they'd left behind, and the roads had been partially cleared. Lights twinkled in the windows of the houses they passed by, and Christmas decorations hung around some of the doors and gables, lifting their spirits.

"The Promised Land," Ryan muttered.

"Are you sure this isn't a mirage?"

He grinned, and felt as though his face might crack, it was so cold.

"Power lines are still up and running. Let's hope the telephone lines are running, too."

"Do you want to try one of these houses?"

Just then, they spotted the welcoming lights of a country pub. With the stars shining overhead and its frontage decked out like a Christmas tree, *The Percy Arms* beckoned to them.

"That has my vote," Ryan said.

"Mine too. Come on, I'll race you there."

The pair of them half-ran, half-slid across the snow-packed road, silly as a pair of schoolchildren, and before Anna could tug open the door to the main bar, Ryan pulled her in for a deep kiss.

"I love you, Doctor Taylor-Ryan."

"Same goes, Chief Inspector. Even with a nose as red as Rudolph's."

* * *

Inside, they were enveloped by the warmth of a roaring fire and the sound of Elton John stepping into Christmas. The main bar was full, and, if Chillingham village had appeared to be a ghost town, there was a good chance that was because most of its residents had decamped to *The Percy Arms,* which served not only as the local drinking hole but as an inn for weary travellers. Although Chillingham Castle had its own generator to make up for any mainline electrical failures, the rest of Chillingham village relied on the National Grid, whose engineers had been unable to access the power lines for nearly forty-eight hours. Without hot water or heating, it was hardly surprising that so many had taken shelter in the nearest village, where electricity was still in abundance and there were beds to spare.

"Hello there!" The landlord called out a friendly greeting from behind the main bar.

"Hi," Ryan said. "We've just walked over from the castle—"

"You're a brave pair," another man remarked, from his position perched on one of the bar stools. "Forecast says we're in for more snow, tonight."

"Well, that's just the problem. We can't get any signal, and our telephone lines are down. We were hoping you might have a telephone we could use?"

"Aye, o' course."

The landlord, who later turned out to be called Mike, folded his arms on the bar.

"Warm yourselves up a bit, first, eh? You look half frozen."

"More than half," Anna joked, as she went about the time-consuming process of unwinding her scarf.

"What can I get the pair of you? A couple of hot apple ciders?"

Tempted though she was, Anna shook her head.

"I'll—ah, I'll just have a hot chocolate."

Ryan considered himself still 'on duty', but since there was no driving to be done, he ordered a half-pint.

"So, you're over from the castle?"

While Anna headed off to the ladies', Ryan leaned against the bar and surveyed his surroundings.

"Yes, we got caught in the snowstorm on Friday night and ended up staying at the castle. Now, we can't get our car out, and the snowdrifts are so high, the roads are completely blocked to vehicles."

"I know," Mike nodded. "Tried heading over there yesterday—my brother farms some of the land out that way. Couldn't get more than half a mile before turning back."

"Do you know if they've opened the A1 again?"

"Nope, it's still shut. Causing pandemonium, since that's the main route into Scotland."

Ryan could imagine the uproar, and looked forward to the fresh caseload of violent crimes that would, no doubt, be waiting for him once he returned to the office.

Mike nodded at Ryan's glass.

"Another?"

"No, better not."

"One for the wife, or is she staying off the booze at the moment?"

Ryan frowned slightly.

"Wha—?"

"My wife was the same, when she was expecting ours. Couldn't stand the smell of it…you alright, lad?"

Ryan cleared his throat.

"She's—ah, Anna's not—"

"Oh, my mistake," Mike said, apologetically. "She had that 'glow', y'see. Must have been the cold weather."

"Yeah, that must be it."

CHAPTER 18

Seated at his desk back at Northumbria Police Headquarters, Detective Constable Jack Lowerson was reeling from an influx of violent crime reported over the festive season. What was it about human nature, he wondered, that led people to lash out during what was supposed to be the happiest time of the year? It didn't matter what faith you ascribed to—Christmas was supposed to be the season of goodwill. But, judging by the list of fresh reports made to the Control Room, it was also the season of grievous bodily harm and manslaughter, many of which were alcohol and drugs-related.

As he was performing an 'eenie-meenie-miney-mo' over which case to pick up next, his desk phone began to ring. He didn't recognise the number on the display screen, but even a chat about PPI claims or a survey about his recent experience buying a washing machine would be preferable to more paperwork.

"Lowerson," he said.

"Jack? It's Ryan."

The young man sat bolt upright in his chair, partly through force of habit when addressed by the man who was his boss, and partly because he was glad to hear from him.

"Ryan! Good to hear from you," he said. "I tried texting you, yesterday, but I guess you were on the road—"

"I haven't been picking up any messages or calls," Ryan said, from his position in the back office of *The Percy Arms*. "Listen, we've got a bit of a situation here."

Lowerson listened, and grew increasingly worried at the thought of his four good friends finding themselves stranded— and even more so when he learned about the murder.

"You're sure it's suspicious?" he asked.

"Pretty sure," Ryan said. "Unless we find a last-minute suicide note in which Carole Black lays out exactly what she planned to do, I'm treating this as murder."

"How can I help?"

Ryan smiled.

"The first issue is getting a forensic team and the coroner's office out here, to take charge of the body, but the roads are completely blocked. Is the A1 still shut?"

"Yes, both directions. The Met Office are keeping the red warning in place."

Damn.

"Alright. Is there any other way of getting up here? What about army vehicles?"

"Leave it with me," Jack said. "I can ring you back."

"Actually, that's the next problem," Ryan said. "I'm calling you from a pub in Chatton because the phone lines are down at the castle and it's a black hole for mobile reception. It took over an hour to walk over here, even though it's only a couple of miles away."

Lowerson didn't like to imagine how cold that walk would have been. Outside, the streets were icy and the air was raw, but he only had to cross the car park.

"It's been in all the news reports," he said. "They're saying it's the worst storm the country's seen in forty years, at least."

"I can believe it," Ryan said. "Look, I need you to run a few background checks for me and gather as much information as you can about the names I'm going to give you."

Lowerson grabbed a pen and some paper.

"Shoot."

Ryan listed all the guests who'd been staying at the castle, as well as its staff members—including the dead woman.

"I'm especially interested in Carole Black's history," he said. "I want to know who she was, and why somebody might want to kill her. I have my suspicions, but that's all they are at the moment."

"Understood. Are you worried there'll be more?"

Ryan thought of all the people he cared about staying under the same roof, and as Anna rounded the corner of the bar, all he wanted to do was keep her away from it all, where he knew she would be safe.

But, as life was teaching him, nowhere was safe from a hunter intent upon the kill.

* * *

While Ryan and Anna prepared themselves for a long journey back to the castle—Anna having politely declined Ryan's suggestion that she stay at *The Percy Arms*—Phillips and MacKenzie made their way back to the Great Hall. They'd spent the better part of the afternoon searching the Estate Office and any other locked room they could find, and had discovered the castle was a rabbit warren of hidden passageways and concealed doors. There was nothing like walking up endless flights of stairs for building up an appetite, and they joined the others at the banqueting table ready to eat with gusto.

Jacqui Baker, her daughter Rosie, and Nadia Halliwell had outdone themselves—or, truth be told, the Baker women had, whilst Nadia helped herself to the wine cellar and watched them from the kitchen bench—producing an Italian feast of breads and pasta.

"I'm allergic to gluten," Sheila said, as they began to tuck in. "Is that pasta gluten-free?"

Jacqui's face fell.

"Oh, dear. I wish you'd mentioned it before…I'm not sure, I just got it from the pantry—let me go and have a look."

"I'm not eating dairy at the moment, either," Sheila said, eyeing the garlic butter and creamy pasta sauce with longing. "It's fattening."

"I'm sure they'll have a tin of tomato soup in the kitchen," MacKenzie snapped. "This looks lovely, Mrs Baker. Thank you."

Jacqui beamed.

"I hope it's alright. I don't usually cook for so many people, do I, Rosie?"

Her daughter shook her head.

"Do you think one of us should take Mr Black a tray?" she asked.

"Yes, that's a good idea—"

"He didn't answer the phone in his apartment," Dodds put in. "I didn't like to disturb him, if he was sleeping."

At that moment, the man himself entered the room, and there was a brief, awkward silence as people scrambled around for something to say.

"Glad you could join us, Samuel," Phillips said. "Why don't you come and sit down beside me, eh? Mrs Baker offered to do the cooking tonight, along with her two helpers."

"I always serve," the man replied, and looked a bit affronted that they'd managed without him. "Usually, dinner isn't until eight."

"I hope you don't mind, but we decided to bring it forward this evening," MacKenzie said. "We thought you'd like to have some time alone."

Samuel looked around the gathered crowd, down at the food, and then thought of Carole's body lying out there in a cold storeroom. People still breathed, and ate, and slept. The world still turned.

And yet…

He couldn't stomach any of it.

"If you'll excuse me, I think I'll go back to my rooms," he muttered.

A moment later, he'd disappeared back into the shadowy hallway, as silently as he had come.

"I'll go and check on him, later on," Dodds said, quietly. "I've known Samuel and Carole ever since I started here at the castle, and he might like a bit of company. I can kip on the sofa in their apartment, if he'd rather not be alone."

MacKenzie nodded, thinking that a victim's closest relatives were often at risk of self-harm in the hours and days following their loved one's death.

"That's a good idea. We understand he hasn't any other family—is that right?"

"Not that I know of," Dodds agreed. "He and Carole never had any kids, and I don't think he was married before. They had each other, really, and that was about it."

The group fell silent, each of them thinking of a loved one they had lost, at one time or another, before Dodds spoke up again.

"Ah, I meant to tell you earlier, but we were distracted by other things…The oil's run out now, for the boiler. You remember, I told you it was running low?"

"Aye, you did," Phillips said. "What do we do about it?"

"I'm afraid we'll have to manage. I've got a few electric heaters, and if we keep the fires stoked up in here, we should be alright, so long as everyone wraps up. The Great Hall is one of the warmest rooms in the house."

"Manage?" Sheila croaked. "How can I be expected to manage? I'm very sensitive to cold weather."

"She's very sensitive," her husband echoed.

Phillips and MacKenzie looked at one another, each feeling glad that the other was not David or Sheila Enfield.

"Try putting another jumper on," Marcus said, biting into a piece of garlic bread. "Or consider emigrating to a warmer climate."

Sheila was rendered momentarily speechless, and Dodds took advantage of the lull in conversation.

"Well, I think I'll go and look out those electric heaters," he said. "I think we have a few knocking around in one of the cupboards downstairs. I'll bring them up."

"Need a hand?" Phillips offered, but Dodds waved him away.

"They're not heavy, and I know what I'm looking for. I'll be back soon."

Once he'd left the room, MacKenzie thought back to Ryan's advice that they should try to stay together, as there was safety in numbers.

"It might be better to camp out in here, just for tonight," she said, and watched them turn to one another in dismay. "I know it isn't what any of us would want, but have you seen the weather outside? The snow's started up again, and we've just learned there'll be no central heating to stave off the chill. There's plenty of room in here for everybody."

And less chance of people wandering about, during the night, she thought.

"Fine by me," Nadia said, and they noticed she was slurring again. She was a slight young woman, whose body was obviously not able to withstand too much alcohol consumption, which was unfortunate since she seemed to like the taste of it so much.

"Which way's the bathroom, again?" she asked, rising unsteadily to her feet. "I think it's this way—"

"Would you like me to come with you?" Rosie offered, half-rising from her chair.

But Nadia had already gone.

"Leave her be," Marcus said lazily. "She spends most of her life half-cut, that one."

"Perhaps you could make sure she's alright," Phillips said, pointedly.

"She's a grown girl."

And they say that chivalry is dead, MacKenzie thought.

"I'll go," she said, and had barely risen from her chair when there came the sound of another blood-curdling scream.

CHAPTER 19

For the second time that day, the guests of Chillingham Castle bolted towards the sound of a woman's scream, moments after the castle clock chimed seven. This time, it came from the direction of the main stairs leading to the courtyard on the ground floor level, which was lit by only a few gas torches and the reflected light from the windows facing the quadrangle.

At the bottom of the stairs, Nadia Halliwell lay in a heap on the floor, with the figure of a man crouched beside her.

Sheila Enfield made a strangled sound in her throat.

"Oh, my God! It's happened again! The murderer's struck *again!*"

The man looked up at that, and held up his hands.

"It's only me!" Dodds called up. "Nadia's taken a fall—twisted her ankle, or maybe broken it."

It was a strange relief to hear Nadia's sharp cry of pain, as Dodds tested the bone.

"Can you walk on it?" he asked, as he helped her up.

Nadia cried out sharply as she tried to put her weight on the ankle she'd injured.

"Ah! No, it hurts too much!"

Without a word, Dodds scooped her up into his arms.

"I'll carry her up to the Grey Apartment," he told them. "Sage? Meet me there, and you can help her get settled."

Marcus, who had been content to watch from the safety of the first floor, made a soft sound of irritation and then stalked off in the direction of their apartment while Dodds carried Nadia carefully across the courtyard towards the south-west tower and up an enclosed spiral staircase. The steps were narrow, but at least they wouldn't be slippery underfoot.

MacKenzie directed the other guests back into the Great Hall, thanking Jacqui Baker for her offer of a cold compress to reduce any swelling, and politely declining Sheila Enfield's offer that she keep 'that poor young woman' company. By her estimation, Nadia had been through enough of an ordeal without being subjected to a lengthy discussion about why Sheila's ailments were far more serious, and far more worthy of attention, than a sprained ankle.

* * *

"Did you hear that?"

Anna turned to Ryan as they rounded the southern edge of the castle.

"It sounded like a scream."

Ryan nodded.

"I heard it too."

He turned to run, but then stopped himself, thinking suddenly of the pub landlord's words earlier that evening.

"Are you—ah, are you managing alright on the snow?"

Anna gave him a quizzical look.

"I've managed all the way to Chatton and back, haven't I?"

"Yes. I was just…checking, I suppose."

"Well, don't worry about me. Let's go and find out what's happened."

All the same, Ryan took her hand and kept a steady pace across the snow, just in case she should fall.

* * *

When Ryan and Anna stepped back into the Great Hall, they found everything topsy-turvy. The shock of Nadia's fall, on top of an already stressful day, had compelled their fellow guests to take MacKenzie's advice and camp out by the fire. Occasional sofas and mattresses had been commandeered from nearby bedrooms and blankets were in the process of being transported from their respective apartments, in preparation.

"Welcome back," Jacqui said, as she made up her bed for the night. "We were starting to worry about you two."

"Made it back in one piece," Ryan said, and squeezed his wife's hand. "We heard a scream?"

"That was Nadia," Rosie explained, tucking her feet up onto an armchair she'd found. "She had one too many again and managed to hurt her ankle. Bill carried her back to her room, and Marcus and your colleagues are in with her now."

"Does she need anything?" Anna asked.

"I took a cold compress through, with some ibuprofen," Jacqui said. "Bill took a look at her ankle and he's put a bandage on it. He's told her to keep it elevated until she can get to the hospital for an x-ray."

"Bad luck," Ryan said.

"Luck's got nothing to do with it," Sheila said, unkindly. "If she'd had a bit more to eat and a bit less to *drink,* then she might not have fallen arse over tit—"

"What's going on around here?" Anna asked, to change the subject. "It looks like you're setting up an air-raid shelter."

"We've run out of oil," Jacqui replied. "The heating's down and so's the hot water, so we're stoking up the fire and the electric heaters and keeping warm in here tonight."

"It wasn't *my* idea," Sheila said. "If you think I want to sleep on a hard sofa surrounded by strangers, you must be mad—"

"Ah, you're back!"

Dodds stepped into the room carrying an electric heater, which he set down while he caught his breath.

"How was the journey?"

Ryan and Anna looked at one another, and thought of the last mile spent walking against the force of the wind, which blew into their eyes and burned their skin as they'd continued to wade through the snow singing *Jingle Bells*.

"Let's just say, it's wasn't a walk in the park."

"Did you have any luck finding a working telephone?" Dodds asked.

Ryan nodded.

"We went to *The Percy Arms*," he said. "Incidentally, the landlord sends his regards."

Dodds grinned.

"Usually like to get down for a couple of pints on my day off," he admitted. "What about the roads? Any news on when the storm's due to pass?"

"The Met Office have renewed their red warning for tonight and tomorrow," Ryan said. "The A1 is still closed between Morpeth and Berwick."

There were murmurs of disappointment around the room.

"And did you manage to get through to your colleagues in CID?"

The room fell quiet, and all heads turned in Ryan's direction.

"Yes," he said. "They'll be joining us as soon as conditions allow. Until then, settle in, because we're in this for the long haul."

CHAPTER 20

Ryan, Anna, Frank and Denise convened back in The Lookout, where they went about the business of boiling water on the stove for a much-needed cup of tea, and turning on the electric radiators they'd been gifted by Bill Dodds, who had taken himself off to check on his friend, Samuel Black.

"He was in a bad way at dinner," Phillips remarked, as he searched for some mugs in the little kitchenette. "I was going to stop in again to see him, but Dodds is probably better placed to lend an ear."

"He said they'd been friends for a couple of years," MacKenzie remarked. "I had the impression Dodds had been working here much longer than that. He seems to know the place inside out."

Ryan came back through to the living room carrying an armful of blankets, which he handed out to each of them as the temperature continued to fall.

"Dodds is a capable man," he remarked. "He did us a good turn, clearing the pathway out of the castle grounds."

"Strong, too," Phillips was bound to say. "Shovelling all that snow, then lifting Nadia up like she was nowt but a feather. Bloke's built like a brick shithouse, as my Da' used to say."

Ryan smiled, marvelling at the poetry of the North-Eastern dialect.

"We heard she fell—is there any possibility she was pushed?"

MacKenzie shook her head.

"She was already unsteady on her feet. In fact, I was about to follow her to the ladies', to make sure she made it in one piece, when we heard her scream. I think it was a simple case of her miscalculating the bottom step and going down hard on her ankle."

"Sage is looking after her, if you can call it that," Phillips said. "The man couldn't care two hoots about that poor lass; it's small wonder she likes a drink."

"You never know what goes on behind closed doors," Anna said, tucking a blanket around her shoulders. "Maybe he's better when they're alone?"

"That's about as likely as Frank being a ballet dancer in his spare time," MacKenzie said, and chuckled when he performed an impromptu pirouette.

For once, Ryan didn't smile.

"I don't think any harm will come to Nadia," he said. "If he'd wanted to hurt her, he'd have done it before now."

The others turned to look at him.

"Who?"

"Marcus Sage, of course."

* * *

They gathered around the electric fire, blankets over their knees and mugs of warm tea in their hands, looking like a group of adult campers preparing to tell ghost stories. Except the story Ryan had to tell them concerned someone very real, and very much alive.

"Sage is the only one who could possibly have done it," Ryan said. "No other explanation makes sense."

"But there were no footprints leading to her body, other than her own," Anna said. "How did he manage it?"

"Are you saying he trod in exactly the same steps, to mask his prints?" Phillips wondered, still looking at things from the wrong direction.

Ryan shook his head.

"Samuel Black has already told us that he and his wife liked to play tricks on their guests," he said. "That's the first and most important clue. Nobody lured Carole out onto the lawn this morning; she walked across to a spot of her choosing, where she knew anybody looking out of the dining room would be able to see her, when they ran to the window. And she was right; we saw her straight away."

"So, she set the scene," Anna said. "How did Sage know she was going to do it? Or, do you think he was an opportunist?"

"I think he was both," Ryan replied, thinking that she would have made an excellent addition to the Criminal Investigation Department. "I think Marcus Sage overheard Carole and her husband planning it, and took a careful note of the details."

"The timing was interesting," MacKenzie said, thoughtfully. "We heard her scream at exactly nine o'clock. I remember, because the clock was chiming the hour."

Ryan nodded.

"It's loud enough to be heard anywhere in the castle, even from the south side. It was a convenient way for Carole and Samuel to plan their stage directions."

"You're saying Marcus Sage got wind of this, somehow," Phillips said. "How did he know she would have a knife?"

"He didn't. Remember, Samuel told us he didn't know anything about the knife. I don't think Carole was the one to supply her own murder weapon; I think Marcus took it off the writing desk in the study and carried it with him when he ran outside."

Ryan paused, cocking his head towards the door to the apartment, but heard only the sound of the wind whistling through the keyhole.

"I think she always planned to scream at around nine o'clock, which Samuel will confirm. Marcus knew it, and he made sure he was within striking distance so he could be the first to run outside to 'help' her. But, instead of falling around laughing at her joke, Marcus pulled out a real knife and finished the job, then tried to act the hero."

"What about the knife?" Anna said. "Won't there be prints on it?"

"There might have been," MacKenzie said. "But I've remembered something interesting that Rosie said in her statement. She said that, when she accidentally grabbed the knife to pull it out, the handle was wet."

Ryan's forehead wrinkled, then cleared again as the answer presented itself.

"Sage washed his prints off with snow," he realised. "He took a handful of snow and rubbed it over the knife handle, to wash away his prints. Clever."

The others imagined the scene he'd just described, and realised he was right. It was the only reasonable explanation.

"That's a very high-risk strategy," Phillips said. "Sage needed to have a good excuse for being on the ground floor, for starters, and then he needed to make sure he was the first one across the lawn. Rosie Baker came a pretty close second; she was less than a minute behind him, and we were only a minute or two behind her."

"He's definitely a risk-taker," Ryan said. "I'm almost certain that's what happened on the lawn this morning, but what I don't yet know is *why*."

"It must be something to do with what she said last night, at the séance," Anna said.

"It seems the most likely reason, but we don't know the significance of 'Elizabeth' or 'Dragfoot' and we've got no means of running even a simple internet search. All we know is that the information was important enough for Sage to want to make sure it never reached the light of day, which is why I'm glad to know that Dodds is going to be spending the night in Samuel's apartment. If Carole found something out and tried to exploit it, there's a chance her husband knew about it too, which makes him a target."

"All this may be true," MacKenzie said. "But we can't prove any of it. There are no witnesses, nothing but circumstantial evidence, unless forensics are able to isolate some trace evidence from the murder weapon."

"I've also asked Lowerson to run thorough checks on all of them, but on Marcus Sage and Carole Black in particular. I want to know the connection because, when we find out the answer to that, we'll find out the reasons she died."

Outside, the castle clock chimed eleven, and Ryan yawned.

"It's been a trek and a half, and I'm exhausted. There's nothing much we can do tonight; the others have safety in numbers and there's a storm raging outside. Marcus Sage is going nowhere."

"Agreed," Phillips said. "I say we make the arrest first thing tomorrow morning, and keep him under lock and key until we can transport him to the nearest station."

The matter decided, they fell into a restless sleep, tossing and turning as the wind seemed to shake the very foundations of the castle.

CHAPTER 21

Sunday

Shortly after eight, Nadia Halliwell awoke to the smell of stale alcohol, which lingered heavily on the cold air of her bedroom and clung to the inside of her mouth and nostrils. Now that the booze had worn off, it no longer numbed the pain in her ankle, which had swollen to the size of a cricket ball and throbbed against the small stack of pillows she'd been using to elevate it. Jacqui Baker had left her a packet of ibuprofen and a jug of water, and she twisted around to slosh some into a glass before swallowing a couple of the pills to take the edge off.

Collapsing back against the pillows, she turned to find the other side of the bed empty, as though it hadn't been slept in.

With a slight frown, she struggled back into a seated position—gasping as the movement jarred her ankle—and looked around the room. Marcus's clothes from the previous two days were still strewn on an occasional chair in the corner of the bedroom, beside the suede dress shoes he'd brought with him to wear at dinner. She heard no sounds coming from the bathroom or the sitting room; only her own laboured breathing as she struggled to remain upright.

Wincing as another shooting pain tore through her ankle, she twisted around again to reach for her mobile phone, which she'd left on the bedside table the night before, and searched for Marcus's number.

But there was no signal, and the call failed to connect.

Thinking she heard footsteps in the corridor outside, Nadia raised her voice to call out.

"*Marcus?* Marcus, is that you?"

But there was no reply.

Across the room, she spotted another phone connected to the castle's internal network, which was still working.

Preparing herself for the pain that would follow, Nadia swung both her legs off the bed and swore loudly as gravity hit her ankle like a ton of bricks. Her skin turned clammy and dark spots swam in front of her eyes, so she took several deep breaths, waiting for the worst to pass before trying to move again.

Once the light-headedness had receded, she grasped the bedpost in both hands.

"Come on," she muttered. "Get up."

With a kind of war cry, she hauled herself upward and managed to hop on her good leg for a couple of paces until she could grab the back of a chair, gritting her teeth against the pain that coursed through her body. Sinking down onto the chair, she allowed herself a few tears of self-pity, and then picked up the phone handset, pressing the speed dial button marked, 'ESTATE OFFICE'.

When it rang out, she felt a frisson of fear, until she remembered that Bill Dodds had been spending the night in Samuel Black's apartment, so she tried the button marked, 'BUTLER' instead.

This time, somebody answered.

* * *

Less than fifteen minutes later, Ryan awoke to a sharp banging on the door.

He sprang up from the sofa, where he'd been sleeping at an awkward angle with Anna tucked against his chest, and opened it to find Bill Dodds standing on the doorstep.

"Bill? What's the matter? Is it Samuel? Nadia?"

Dodds shook his head.

"No, they're both alright. Well, she's in pain, but—anyway, I'm not here about her. It's Marcus. We can't find him anywhere."

Ryan's eyes turned flat.

"How long has he been missing?"

"I've no idea," Dodds replied. "Nadia was dead to the world throughout the night, and she only woke up twenty minutes ago to find him gone. She thought he might have been in the Great Hall or in one of the other main rooms, but I've had a look and he isn't there."

"Alright. We need to organise a search party. Gather everyone in the Great Hall and I'll join you in five minutes."

Dodds nodded, and hurried back down the spiral staircase and across the courtyard to see it done.

"Who was that?" Anna asked, rubbing sleep from her eyes.

"Bill Dodds. It's Marcus—he's missing."

"Missing?" MacKenzie said. "What? *When?*"

"We're not sure," Ryan said, lacing up his shoes. "Nadia woke up to find him gone."

"He can't have gone far, in this weather," Phillips said. "Where would he go, on foot?"

"I don't know, Frank. All I know is, we could have collared him last night, but we didn't. That's my fault."

"It was a well-reasoned decision that we all agreed with," MacKenzie said. "That's a different thing entirely. Anyway, Frank's right. If the bastard's made a run for it, he can't have gone very far."

* * *

Ryan asked Phillips and MacKenzie to take a walk around the perimeter of the castle, to see whether there were any fresh tracks in the snow to indicate the direction Marcus Sage had taken. While they did that, he and Anna made their way back to the Great Hall, where they found the other guests in a state of heightened anxiety.

"What's this all about?" David Enfield asked. "Dodds told us to stay in here on police orders, but he hasn't told us why. What the hell's going on?"

"It's come to our attention that one of your party is missing," Ryan said. "Given the extreme weather conditions outside, our main priority is to ensure Mr Sage hasn't succumbed to exposure somewhere in the castle grounds—"

He broke off, as Phillips and MacKenzie entered the room, their cheeks pink from their exertions outside.

"No tracks anywhere around the castle perimeter," Phillips told him. "We walked a full circle, but there was no sign. The outbuildings are locked too."

"That makes things much simpler," Ryan said, turning back to address the room. "Mr Sage must still be somewhere inside the castle. I'd like to ask for volunteers to help us search the place from top to bottom, working in pairs."

Slowly, all hands were raised apart from Sheila and David Enfield—who remained resolutely silent—and Nadia Halliwell, who was unable to walk.

"Thanks," Ryan said. "Alright, Jacqui and Rosie, take the north-east corner, please. Bill and Samuel, please take the south-east. Denise, Frank, you take the north-west, while Anna and I take the south-west. Mr and Mrs Enfield, since you'd rather not join us in the search, can I ask you to keep the fire burning and check to see if Miss Halliwell has all she needs?"

After receiving a grudging nod, Ryan clapped his hands.

"Alright, let's get going. If anybody finds anything of interest, just holler until somebody comes."

With that, they scattered to the four corners of the castle and began the hunt for Marcus Sage.

CHAPTER 22

After half an hour, Ryan began to worry.

"Maybe he managed to get out another way, or perhaps Phillips and MacKenzie missed his tracks—they can be difficult to spot, when fresh snow is falling all the time."

"Possibly, but Frank and Denise aren't likely to miss anything like that," Anna said. "They're too experienced."

Ryan nodded, and checked inside the wardrobe in one of the bedrooms.

"How many bedrooms does this make?"

"God only knows," she replied. "They all merge into one, after a while."

Anna admired the delicate carvings on the bed, then crouched down to check underneath it.

"What does Marcus hope to achieve by running or hiding?" she wondered aloud. "His entire plan was risky, and he strikes me as the kind of man to brazen it out for as long as possible. He must know that you don't have any real evidence against him."

"*Yet,*" Ryan said. "That might follow, so long as we can get Faulkner up here before the physical evidence deteriorates any further."

They moved to the spiral staircase and wound their way up to the top level and what was known as the 'King Edward I Room'. Before her untimely death, Carole had indulged Anna's love of history and given them both a brief lecture about the rooms in the castle, so they knew this was the most ancient of all the state rooms. In days gone by, the Lords of the castle were tucked safely away from lesser mortals—and their stench—and this particular room had enabled the visiting monarch of the day in 1298 to rest himself on his way to Scotland, where he famously captured William Wallace.

Braveheart, to any fans of Mel Gibson.

Where once there might have been guards of honour patrolling the upper gallery level of the room, now there was only an empty space.

"Nowhere to hide in here," Ryan said.

Before Anna could reply, they heard the frantic banging of a dinner gong in the courtyard outside.

"At last!" he said, and the pair of them hurried back down the spiral staircase to see who'd managed to find their missing murderer.

People swarmed from all four towers to see who was banging the gong, and they found it was Rosie Baker. She stood at the northern end of the courtyard, nearest the front doors and beside the entrance to what was called the 'still room'—impossible to miss in a bright pink bobble hat and multicoloured scarf. As Ryan drew near, he could see she looked thoroughly shaken up.

It was, after all, the second dead body she'd had the misfortune to see that weekend.

* * *

"Rosie?"

Ryan put a steadying hand on her arm, and spoke with urgency so she was forced to focus on his words, and not on the memory of what she'd seen.

"My mum's in there with him," she managed. "The oubliette. In there."

She waved a hand towards the Still Room and, beyond it, to the Dungeon. It was, perhaps, the most storied room in any self-respecting castle, and this one was no different. Ryan asked Anna to lead the other guests back to the Great Hall, and then made his way through to what had once been a place of terrible violence.

As he entered the Armoury, he was taken aback to find Jacqui Baker standing at one end of the room, staring down at an old throne-like chair, with spikes protruding from its seat and back. Whichever poor unfortunate seated themselves on it was bound to get a nasty surprise, but he wasn't concerned with the many weird and wonderful collector's items in the castle; he was more concerned with the people sheltering under its mighty roof.

"Jacqui?"

When she turned around, he guessed she'd been crying until very recently.

"I was—I was only wondering, how bad did a person have to be, to be pushed down onto this chair?" she whispered.

"I think it was a more arbitrary process back then," Ryan said. "If you were Scottish and came a-knockin' around these parts, there was a good chance you'd end up being hanged, drawn and quartered, thrown in the oubliette, or tortured for information. It came with the territory."

She nodded mutely.

"He's—Marcus is through there, in the oubliette," she said. "At first, we almost missed him, because you can't see much of him for the rubble."

"The rubble?" Ryan asked, and then remembered the warning they'd been given about not entering the Dungeon because one of the interior walls had given out, and was in need of repair.

"He's dead," she added, in the same emotionless voice. "The last time I saw somebody dead, it was my husband."

Ryan heard the grief, and could empathise. Every time he stood over the bodies of the dead, he thought of those they left behind, of the kind of person they might have been, given the chance. He grieved for all of them—good or bad—and stood in solidarity with those who remained.

It had taken Phillips and MacKenzie a few minutes longer to walk back from the top of their tower, thanks to an old injury in her leg which flared up badly in cold weather, but now they stepped inside the Dungeon to join them.

"Hello—found something?"

"Yes, I was about to take a quick look, but I think Mrs Baker needs to go and be with her daughter—"

MacKenzie needed no second bidding.

"Come on, Jacqui, let's go and find Rosie and see if we can rustle up a nice cuppa. That's just what the doctor ordered, isn't it?

They heard her chatter away to the woman through the Still Room and out into the courtyard, putting her at ease with her unpretentious nature and unthreatening manner.

Marcus Sage could have learned a lot from Denise MacKenzie.

Unfortunately, it was too late for him to learn anything else at all, since he now lay face up on a pile of rubble which, at first glance, appeared to have fallen from the half-collapsed stone wall on the lower half of the oubliette. As far as places to forget people went, it was a fine example, being little more than a hole in the ground where enemies of the Lord, or of his king, had once been thrown—left to rot inside the claustrophobic space surrounded by the remains of those who had gone before.

It was a place of untold horror, even now, where it ought to have been nothing more than a museum relic.

"Good God," Phillips said. "How the heck did he wind up in there? D'you think he took a wrong turn and fell sometime in the night? Maybe he thought it was a good place to hide, but forgot the wall was unstable."

"Too early to say," Ryan muttered, straightening up from where he'd been bending over to peer down into the small, shadowy hole. "It's too dark to see properly. There must be another access down there, so we can get a better look at him."

Phillips was eager to get out of there, especially since a slight odour of decomposition was already rising up to assault his nostrils, telling them he'd been dead much longer than just a couple of hours.

"I'll go and ask Dodds," he said, and bolted out the door before Ryan could say 'scaredy-cat'.

CHAPTER 23

The only way to access the lower half of the oubliette was from outside.

Bill Dodds found the appropriate key in the Estate Office and led them out of the castle via the south doors so that they could pick up some shovels on the way past the stables, skirting around the walls until they came to the front of the castle on the north side.

"The gate to access the oubliette is behind there," Dodds said, pointing to a snowdrift to the left of the main doors. "Let's shovel some of the snow away and see if we can get it open."

The three men worked for ten minutes to clear a path, and then Dodds set his shovel aside and selected an ornate iron key hanging from his chain and slipped it into the lock. The mechanism still worked, but it was clear the old gate hadn't been used in a very long time, and it let out a long, metallic whine in protest.

Ryan crouched down to look at the scene awaiting him on the other side.

The man who had been Marcus Sage lay in the pit of the oubliette, arms outstretched, in a cruciform position. Only parts of his face and torso were visible beneath a small mountain of rubble, pieces of which were the size of small boulders. Blood was spattered all over the dusty floor—presumably from where the boulders had connected with skin and bone—but otherwise there were no visible footprints or any signs of human interference.

"Poor bugger," Phillips said. "He must've panicked, and tried to make a run for it during the night. Hard to see a hole that size, if you're not looking for it."

Ryan would usually have agreed with him. The staging of the body seemed to tell the story of a man who'd been poking around somewhere he shouldn't, and had paid the ultimate price.

And yet…

"Look again, Frank."

Dodds peered through the open doorway, too, and sucked in a sharp breath.

"Horrible way to die," he muttered. "And a big price to pay, for being careless. We *told* people not to go in there. It's the most haunted part of the castle, if you believe in all that stuff, so it's usually very popular with the ghost hunting crowd. Part of the wall is starting to give way, though, and we've been trying to repair it, so the area's been closed off to the public for a few months. There should have been a yellow 'DANGER' sign on the wall outside, to remind visitors."

Ryan said nothing, and drew out his phone to take photographs of the scene, for the second time in as many days.

"Have you spotted it yet, Frank?" he murmured, as he snapped pictures.

"Spotted what?" Dodds asked.

"The reason we know that Marcus didn't die accidentally," Ryan said.

Dodds fell silent, studying the scene alongside Phillips

"He's lying face-up," Phillips realised, suddenly.

"Exactly," Ryan said, with a smile.

"What difference does that make?" Dodds wondered.

"It makes all the difference," Ryan said. "Between a ruling of accidental death and murder, for one thing. Forensic scientists have reached a stage where they can tell police teams how a body fell, and with what kind of force. For instance, when a person is walking along and they fall through a manhole accidentally, they 'step fall', and gravity means they'd tend to land face-down."

Dodds nodded.

"I see. So, from the way he's lying now, you can work out the most likely way he fell?"

"Sure. For instance, I can tell from the way his legs are bunched up at the side, and from the way his arms are splayed, that Mr Sage was lowered into the manhole and then dropped."

Dodds shot him a surprised look.

"But...if you think Marcus Sage has been murdered, or something of that kind, what does that mean for Carole? I assumed you were looking for him because you suspected him of having murdered Carole, but, if that's true and he's a killer, then...who killed *him?*"

"That's very much the question," Ryan said, as he continued to snap pictures, noting the lack of footprints in the fine layer of dust that had settled itself on the body and in a perfect circle around it.

"Why'd you tell him all that?" Phillips asked, once the Estate Manager had left them to document the scene.

"Because I want him to pass it on to the others. I want whoever did this to know that *I* know," Ryan replied. "Whoever we're dealing with thinks they've been very clever, Frank. I want them to know that we're not as stupid as they seem to think."

Phillips grinned.

"They never seem to learn, do they?"

"Not so far."

Phillips blew on his cold fingers and nodded towards Marcus.

"How long d'you reckon he's been dead?" he asked.

"Must be several hours, at least. He's as stiff as a board, and there's an odour despite the fact it's as cold as a fridge down here."

"Around midnight, or thereabouts?"

Ryan nodded.

"There's nothing unusual on his body that I can see. He's wearing a coat, and I think I can see a smashed torch amongst the rubble—nice touch, there, to add weight to the theory he was out walking and managed to fall."

"Shame there isn't a smashed watch," Phillips said. "At times like these, it'd help to have an accurate time of death."

Ryan stood up and stretched out his back.

"Sadly, that only happens on the Orient Express," he joked. "We'll have to do things the hard way, Frank."

* * *

The "hard way" meant legwork, and lots of it.

They began by interviewing Nadia Halliwell, the closest thing they had to Marcus's next of kin. The woman who had been Marcus Sage's sometime paramour was still laid up in bed, where she was enjoying the maternal attentions of Jacqui Baker and Sheila Enfield, both of whom fussed around her with blankets, cups of tea and more information about their neighbours and pets than she would ever wish to know. When Ryan and Phillips entered her apartment, they found Nadia looking as pale as the pillows where she lay.

"Do you mind if we come in for a chat?" Ryan asked.

Nadia shook her head, eager for conversation—any conversation—that didn't involve Sheila's pedigree cockapoo, who, she told them, went by the name of His Lordship.

Ryan dispatched Jacqui and Sheila with as much charm as he could muster.

"I heard Marcus is dead," she said. "Is it true?"

"Yes, I'm sorry."

"How did he die?"

Rocky ground, Ryan thought.

"He appears to have fallen into the oubliette," he replied.

Nadia closed her eyes and shook her head, turning an even whiter shade of pale.

"That's—God, that's terrible. How did it happen? Did he fall?"

"I don't think so," Ryan said simply.

It took a couple of seconds, but then the import of his statement hit home.

"You think—you think somebody *pushed him?*"

"That's a possibility."

"But—why? Who would want to?"

"We were hoping you might be able to help answer those questions," Ryan said.

"I don't know anything," she replied, and tears leaked down her face. "It's my fault. If we'd never come here, he'd still be alive."

Ryan handed her a tissue from the dressing table nearby, and dragged a chair over to sit beside her.

"Let's start at the beginning," he said gently. "Why don't you start by telling us how you came to know Marcus?"

"You mean, how we met? It was in one of his wine bars— *Shellfish and Champagne.* He's a big name on the club and restaurant scene; he owns quite a few of them in the centre of Newcastle and one or two in Durham. People knew him."

"And did they like him?"

She was caught off-balance, unsure of what to say for the best.

"The truth is always preferable," Ryan said, helpfully.

"Well…the thing is, Marcus had a lot of money, and he had a certain manner…I suppose you'd say he liked things how he liked them. He preferred to have the best of everything, and people didn't always like that."

She pulled a face.

"I suppose I thought he was strong, you know? Confident, because he was a self-made man. At first, he was really romantic, as well. He used to send me flowers."

"Was it his idea to come here to Chillingham?" Ryan asked. He remembered Sage's version of events, but was interested to know if Nadia's recollection would be the same.

"It was my idea," she said. "I suppose I'd started to notice he was cooling off a bit, and I thought it might give us a little boost to have a festive weekend away, so I booked it—well, actually, the castle sent me some prize vouchers, and I decided to use them."

"When was this, Nadia?"

"Oh, maybe three or four months ago? The voucher arrived in the post and all I had to do was confirm the booking by sending an email to the hospitality team."

Ryan didn't recall seeing a hospitality team listed on the 'ABOUT US' section of the castle's directory, and he filed that little nugget away for later.

"How long had you been seeing one another, Nadia?"

"Since around February," she said. "About ten months."

"And were you happy together?"

Her eyes fell away.

"No, I don't think we were," she admitted. "He was cruel at times, and I drink too much. But how many people are really happy together, Chief Inspector? How many people can truly call themselves 'happy'? There's always fighting and cheating... or cheating and fighting. Not everybody gets the fairy tale."

Only a lucky few, Ryan thought, and was grateful every day to be one of them.

"There'll be someone else, lass," Phillips told her. "Maybe, someone better, eh? Nice girl like you deserves a decent bloke."

Her chin wobbled and, after giving her a minute to collect herself, Ryan continued.

"Now, I'm going to ask you to turn your mind back to the events of last night," he said. "Can you start by telling us how you hurt your ankle?"

Just at the mention of it, she felt a twinge of pain run up her leg.

"I had too much wine," she said, honestly. "I know I did, and I accept that I'm laid up here because my faculties were impaired.

If I'd taken things more slowly, and been more aware of where I was stepping, I might never have fallen. I'm just lucky I didn't break my neck."

"Could've happened to anybody," Phillips said, kindly.

She shuffled a little higher in the bed, trying to get comfortable.

"Do you need anything?" Ryan asked. "Water? Tablets?"

"Gin and tonic?" she said. "Sorry, bad joke. You asked me how the accident happened…well, to be honest, I can't remember what time it was or anything like that, but I know that I went off to look for the ladies' room. There's one near the Great Hall or in the apartment here, but in my…ah, slightly woozy state, I decided it was a good idea to go to the one on the ground floor, near the kitchen, because it was the first one that came to mind," she said, with a shrug.

"Anyway, I missed the bottom step on the way down the main stairs and went down hard on my ankle. I'm pretty sure I heard it crack."

Phillips pulled a face, having broken enough bones in his life to recognise the sound.

"I think I might have hit the back of my head, too, because I blacked out for a second and, when I came around, Bill Dodds was beside me, squeezing my hand and asking if I was okay."

"Were you alone on the stairs until then, Nadia?"

She nodded.

"I didn't see anyone else at all."

"Okay. What happened next?"

"I must have screamed, because I heard everyone rushing out and Mrs Enfield shouting something like, 'It's happening again!'. I don't remember what else was said, but I know that Mr Dodds carried me back here, and Marcus helped to get me into bed."

"Do you know what time that was, Nadia?"

"Sorry, I have no idea. Mrs Baker gave me some ibuprofen and some water, I took them, and then I fell asleep. I suppose you could ask Jacqui what time she brought the tablets through."

"How's your foot now?" Phillips asked.

"Really sore," she admitted, lifting back the covers to reveal the swollen skin. "Bill put a field bandage on it for me, but I really need to have it x-rayed. Do you know when the roads will be open again?"

"No word yet," Ryan replied. "We'll make sure you get all the right treatment, as soon as we can."

She nodded, and looked down at her hands.

"Is it wrong that I don't really miss him?" she whispered suddenly. "Shouldn't I feel…*more?*"

"Perhaps your heart knew sooner than your head that Marcus wasn't the right person for you," Phillips said.

"That's a kind way of putting it," she smiled. "It's a shame you're already spoken for, Sergeant."

Phillips turned a slow, uncomfortable shade of red, much to Ryan's amusement.

"Do you remember anything else from last night, Nadia?" he asked, to give Phillips a reprieve. "Do you remember what time Marcus left the apartment?"

She began to shake her head, and then looked up.

"I think Marcus took a call on the castle phone sometime during the night," she said. "It sort of woke me up but I was so sleepy, I couldn't keep my eyes open."

"Do you remember what was said?"

"No, but I remember Marcus's voice sounding a bit sharp, and then he said something to me about going out, but I was dozing off at that point."

Ryan tried a different tack.

"You've already told us that Marcus owned some clubs around Newcastle," he said. "Do you know anything else about how he made his money? Did he run any businesses, for example?"

"Marcus was a very private person," she said. "He never told me anything about his business affairs. I think he thought I looked nice on his arm, but that's about it."

She laughed without mirth.

"Story of my life."

"It doesn't have to be," Ryan said smoothly. "Do you know of anyone who might have wanted to kill Marcus? Did he have any enemies?"

She seemed surprised.

"He might have had professional rivals, but I don't know of anybody who'd have wanted to kill him."

"What about the other guests—did he mention knowing any of them before coming to stay here?"

Nadia shook her head firmly.

"Not at all," she replied. "I think he found them all hard work, for different reasons."

"You're sure he never mentioned having any connection with Carole Black, for example?"

Nadia shook her head again.

"He never mentioned a thing to me about it."

"Alright, Nadia, we're very grateful for your help, I've just got one more question for you."

He took out his phone and brought up a picture of the torch that had been found on the floor, near Marcus's head.

"Is this yours?"

She peered at the photograph, then nodded.

"Marcus bought that last minute from a petrol station on the way over here. We were a bit disorganised in bringing the things we might need for the ghost tour," she explained. "He must have taken it with him."

Both men thanked her and wished her a speedy recovery.

"What will happen now?" she asked, looking between them with frightened eyes. "If somebody wanted to hurt Marcus, do you think they'd want to hurt me, too?"

"We have no reason to think that, Miss Halliwell, but, until we've completed our investigation, we'll be advising everybody to remain vigilant."

As they reached the door, Ryan turned back.

"You said a prize voucher arrived in the post—which prize did you enter?"

"I don't know—I assumed I'd been entered into some sort of automatic draw. I'm sorry, I never asked…is it important?"

Ryan smiled.

"Probably nothing to worry about. Get well soon, Miss Halliwell."

But, as the door shut behind them, she cast her eyes around the empty apartment, and was afraid.

CHAPTER 24

MacKenzie set up a makeshift interview room in one of the smaller state rooms adjoining the Great Hall, and appointed Anna as Unofficial Helper—or Crowd Enforcer, as the case may be. Tensions were running at an all-time high following the discovery of a second body, with panic threatening to take hold. This was never more evident than when they spoke to Sheila Enfield, who had volunteered to be interviewed first, so far treating the experience much as she would a good trip to the hairdressers—namely, as an ideal opportunity to gossip.

"…and I can tell you that Jacqui Baker snores like a trooper," she was saying, as she nibbled a packet of beefy Hula-Hoops. "It's a wonder any of us got any sleep at all, last night."

"I understand you shared the Great Hall with several people last night, Mrs Enfield. Can you tell me who was with you?"

Sheila heaved a sigh.

"Well, I was on a sofa, and David was on the floor because he knows I get a bad back," she said. "Then, there was Jacqui and Rosie, who had the armchair and the other sofa. I think Mr Dodds was staying with Mr Black in his apartment, and Marcus and Nadia were in their own room after she twisted her ankle."

She leaned forward, conspiratorially.

"It's a mercy she didn't break her neck! Well, I don't need to tell *you,* Detective. You saw what she was like, last night."

MacKenzie merely smiled.

"Tell me, Mrs Enfield, what time did you fall asleep—roughly?"

"It must have been around ten," she replied. "I had a game of cards with Jacqui, we chatted for a little while and then I curled up on the sofa and tried to sleep."

"What did you talk about?"

"Oh, this and that," Sheila said. "We were both a bit overwrought, and we decided to have a glass of wine before bed. That probably didn't help her snoring."

"I see. And did you see or hear anything unusual during the course of the evening—aside from the snoring," MacKenzie added, before Sheila could.

"No, nothing whatsoever."

"Had you met any of your fellow guests prior to staying at the castle?"

"No, they were complete strangers to me. Why do you ask?"

MacKenzie ignored the question and ploughed on, while the going was good.

"How about Mr Sage?" she pressed. "Had you seen or heard his name before meeting him on Friday?"

Sheila looked her dead in the eye and shook her head.

"I'd never heard of the man."

* * *

"Well, I have to say, I didn't really sleep very well last night," Jacqui Baker said, a few minutes later.

"Because of the cold?" MacKenzie asked.

"That didn't help but, actually, it was because of Sheila Enfield's snoring. It was very loud, and she was lying on her back, so that wouldn't help."

"I'm sorry to hear that," MacKenzie said, and looked down at her notepad, to gather her composure.

Oh, to have been a fly on the wall…

"Could you talk me through your movements last night, after dinner?"

"Well, Mr Dodds and Mr Black took care of the washing up, which was nice. I'd done the cooking, if you remember, and I was feeling a little tired, by then. Well now…after Nadia hurt her ankle, I took her a cold compress and some tablets I had in my bag to help reduce the swelling. Such a shame, what's happened to her, and especially now she won't have Marcus to help her."

"Do you happen to remember what time it was, when Nadia hurt her ankle?"

"Yes, actually I do. It was exactly seven o'clock, because I remember the castle clock chiming the hour."

MacKenzie made a note.

"And when did you last see Mr Sage?"

"That would be when I dropped off the tablets for Nadia…it was around twenty past seven, I think. I didn't see him after then, so I guessed he was tired or too busy looking after his girlfriend to come and socialise."

"And who did you socialise with?"

"Well, I had a nice chat and a game of cards with Sheila, although she gets a bit competitive whereas I prefer to play just for fun. Each to their own," she said quickly. "Rosie was reading a book, and David Enfield was dozing on the sofa for a while, until Sheila made a bit of a song and dance about needing that particular sofa to sleep on."

"Had you met the Enfields before you came here, Mrs Baker?"

"No, not at all."

"How about any of the other guests—or the staff?"

"You know, it's funny...I thought something about Mr Sage was familiar, but I can't for the life of me think of where I'd have seen him before. I think he must have one of those faces."

"If you happen to remember, please come and let one of us know," Mackenzie said. "It might be important."

Jacqui nodded.

"One final question then, Mrs Baker. Do you remember seeing or hearing anything unusual during the night?"

"No, nothing."

* * *

"Please take a seat, Mr Dodds."

The Estate Manager settled himself on a chair opposite MacKenzie, while Anna watched quietly from the corner of the room.

"It's been a strange few days, hasn't it?" MacKenzie said. "I want to thank you for all your help with our investigation so far."

Dodds waved that away.

"Happy to help however I can. To be perfectly honest, I'm still reeling after Carole's death, and now we have another to contend with. I can't wrap my head around it."

"Perhaps you could start by telling me when you took up your post as Estate Manager, here at Chillingham?"

"About two years ago," he said. "I saw the job advertised in the *Morpeth Herald* and thought I'd give it a go."

"Did you know any of the staff here, before you started?"

"No," he said. "But Carole and Samuel were always very friendly. They made me feel like part of the family. I'll always be grateful to them for that."

He looked down at his hands, to mask the sheen of tears.

"What about the other guests? Did you know any of them before?"

"No, I didn't."

"What about Mr Sage? How did you find him?"

Dodds raised his eyebrows, then gave a light shrug.

"Not my kind of bloke. Too much of a poser, for a start," he said, with the twist of a smile. "Didn't like the way he treated women."

There was a hard tone to his voice they hadn't heard before.

"Nadia's a nice woman," MacKenzie said, meaningfully.

"Yes, she is."

When nothing more was forthcoming, she moved onto the next question.

"Talk me through your movements last night, Bill. Where did you go? What did you do?"

"Ah…well, let me see now. I saw you all at dinner, then I left just before seven to go and find the electric heaters after the boilers packed in. I was just about to carry the first one up to the Great Hall, when I heard Nadia scream. She'd hurt her ankle at the bottom of the stairs, so I ran over to see if she was alright. She's lucky it wasn't a lot worse."

MacKenzie nodded.

"How did Mr Sage seem to you, when you last saw him?"

"The last time I saw him was in their bedroom, in the Grey Apartment. He seemed irritated," Dodds said. "He didn't seem to like the inconvenience of having to look after his girlfriend, but…hey, it's none of my business."

"Did he appear to have anything else on his mind? Did he seem concerned, at all?"

"If he was, he didn't look it, and he certainly didn't tell me about it."

MacKenzie nodded. "What did you do, after you'd carried Nadia back to the Grey Apartment?"

"I fetched the first aid kit from the kitchen, where Mrs Baker was already sorting out a cold compress for her ankle. We went back together, I bandaged the ankle as best I could, then I left them to it and headed back downstairs to finish lugging those electric heaters upstairs. That's when I ran into Ryan and Anna in the Great Hall"—he smiled over at the lady herself, who smiled politely in return—"and asked them how their journey to Chatton went. After that, I decided to head to the kitchen and help with the washing up, and I found Samuel already there. I guess he was finding comfort in familiar things."

Dodds sighed, and rubbed the back of his neck.

"We took care of the dishes, then I offered to spend the night on his sofa if he wanted the company, which he did."

"What time did you head back to his apartment?"

"Must've been around nine, or thereabouts. Samuel and I stayed up till about midnight or thereabouts, reminiscing about Carole, talking. Next thing I know, it's the morning, and I get a call from Nadia asking if I know where Marcus has gone. The rest, I think you know."

MacKenzie made another quick note, then set her pen down.

"Did you stay in Samuel's apartment all night?" she asked.

Dodds nodded.

"Could you speak up, for the recording, please?"

"Oh, sorry. Yes, I stayed in his apartment all night, until the phone started ringing. That was Nadia, asking me if I knew where Marcus had got to."

"During the night, did you hear or see anything untoward?"

He shook his head.

"Nothing. Samuel went to his bed, I kipped on the sofa, and that was about it."

CHAPTER 25

While MacKenzie and Anna interviewed the remaining guests, Ryan prepared to make the journey into Chatton for a second time.

"I could come with you for a bit of company?" Phillips offered.

But Ryan shook his head.

"I'll be quicker on my own, and, more importantly, I need you to stay here in case..."

"In case?"

"Just, in case."

Phillips' lips flattened.

"They'll have to get through me first. You can rely on that, lad."

Ryan put a hand briefly on his friend's shoulder, in silent thanks. It would make his task all the easier, knowing he could trust Phillips to watch over all that was most important to him in the world.

"The phones are still down, and I agreed to call Lowerson at midday," he said, tugging on his gloves. "I'm hoping he'll have done those background checks, because Marcus Sage died for a reason, and we won't find it out from any of *them*."

"That's as maybe," Phillips said. "Trouble is, they've all got an alibi, as far as I can see. Samuel was in with Bill, the Enfields and the Bakers were in the Great Hall, and Nadia couldn't have gone more than three steps, let alone lure Marcus all the way down to the Dungeon and shove him into the oubliette."

"I think he was dragged there, from another spot," Ryan put in. "There were drag marks on the back of his heels."

"Well, that just proves it. There's no way that slip of a lass could have dragged *herself* anywhere, let alone a six-foot dead weight. You saw how bad she was, earlier on."

Ryan nodded.

"I agree, nobody could get far with an injury like that."

"Which brings us back to the point," Phillips said. "It had to be one of them, but if they're all alibied, it couldn't have been *any* of them."

"Unless it was all of them," Ryan said.

Phillips simply stared.

"Bloody hell," he said.

"You see why I can't leave Anna alone here," Ryan said. "Denise, either, for that matter. I know how strong they are, I know they'd fight, but they could be outnumbered. Sometimes, it's a numbers game, and I don't like leaving them a man down."

Phillips looked his friend in the eye.

"I'll make myself count for two," he said, and Ryan smiled.

"You count for a hundred good men in my book, Frank. There's nobody I'd rather be trapped in a snowy haunted castle with, and nobody I trust more when my back's against the wall."

He grasped the door handle, hesitated, then turned back to give his friend a hard, back-slapping hug.

"Godspeed," Phillips muttered.

* * *

As Ryan set off into the snow, Samuel Black shuffled into the interview room bearing a small tray of coffee and biscuits, which he set on the table. MacKenzie thanked him and, when he continued to stand awkwardly, she realised he was waiting for her to invite him to sit.

"Please, take a seat, Mr Black."

He did, perching himself on the very edge of the chair and linking his hands in his lap.

"We'd like to offer our condolences once again for your loss, Samuel," MacKenzie said quietly. "DCI Ryan has made the proper authorities aware and they'll be attending with the coroner, at the very earliest opportunity."

He nodded, but made no comment.

"You're aware that Mr Sage was found dead this morning, in the oubliette?"

Samuel's face displayed no emotion whatsoever.

"Yes, Bill told me."

"We're trying to build a picture of where everybody was last night, Mr Black. Could you start by telling me your movements, please? I know that you briefly came to join us for dinner and then changed your mind. What did you do, then?"

He sighed heavily.

"I wasn't hungry," he said. "I couldn't face eating, not when Carole is lying out there in the storeroom."

"We understand," she assured him. "You've had a terrible shock."

"I—well, I sort of…I suppose I wandered around for a while," he said, in an embarrassed tone. "I walked around the castle polishing the furniture. It gave me something to do with my hands."

"Distraction can be a good thing," she agreed. "Then what?"

"I went back to my apartment, but everything…it just reminds me of her," he said. "I heard a scream at around seven o'clock, and I ran out to see what had happened. Everything seemed to be in hand, so I decided to make myself useful and start the washing up. Mrs Baker came in not long after to make up a cold compress for Miss Halliwell, then Bill joined me and helped out in the kitchen."

"Have you known Mr Dodds for a long time?"

"It seems like it sometimes, but no. Bill joined the team a couple of years ago and he fit straight into our way of life here. Not everybody is suited to it, but he seems to be."

"He's your friend?"

"Yes, certainly. Last night, we had a couple of whiskeys—I talked, and he listened."

"What did you talk about?"

"Land, horses, life at the castle…and Carole. Mostly, Carole. I talked about her, and he indulged me. He said it was food for the soul to remember the good things."

He sounds like he knows what he's talking about," MacKenzie said.

Samuel inclined his head.

"Though he hasn't spoken of it, I heard on the grapevine that Bill's wife committed suicide many years ago."

Two suicides in one group, MacKenzie thought. *Interesting.*

"Did either you or Mr Dodds leave your apartment at any time during the night?"

"No. It was far too cold to be roaming around the castle at that hour, especially as the heating was down. As for Bill, I'm a light sleeper and the door has a very squeaky hinge, so I do think I'd have heard him."

Once the interview was concluded, MacKenzie turned to her friend with a baffled expression. It was touching to think of the two men supporting one another through their private grief, but it presented a big problem for their investigation.

"They all have an alibi," Anna said, hitting the nail on the head.

MacKenzie nodded thoughtfully.

"One of them could conceivably have snuck out of the Great Hall—or, either Bill or Samuel could have waited until the other was asleep and taken the chance to slip out of the apartment—but it's highly risky, and the question is…how would they lure Marcus out of his apartment and down to the Dungeon without alerting Nadia?"

* * *

"The phone call."

MacKenzie's question was answered by Phillips, when he popped his head around the door a short time later.

"What? The phone lines are down…there haven't been any—"

"No, I'm on about the internal system," Phillips explained. "When we interviewed her, Nadia said she remembers Marcus taking a call sometime during the night, and then him telling her he'd be heading out. She was away with the fairies at that point, so she doesn't remember anything else about what was said, or who he was talking to, but it would explain how they got him out of the apartment and on his own."

"There's a telephone in most of the rooms," Anna said. "There's one on the dresser in the Great Hall, and we know there's one in Samuel's apartment, because it's listed as a 'speed dial' and Nadia used it this morning."

"But how could anybody have used them, without being overheard by one of the other guests?" MacKenzie asked.

She stood up and paced over to the window, where she saw a single track of footprints leading off to the east along the pathway Dodds had dug out the previous day, and surmised correctly that Ryan had left to walk back into Chatton.

"What if—no, that's probably silly," Anna murmured.

"You've never made a silly suggestion in the five years I've known you," Phillips said. "What were you thinking of?"

"I was only wondering…what if they all did it?"

Phillips hadn't intended to discuss Ryan's theory, in case it might cause her to be worried, but he should have known Anna would be on the same wavelength.

"If you ever fancy a job down at CID, there'll be a desk waitin' for you," he chuckled. "Ryan was suggesting the very same thing, just before he set off for Chatton."

Anna's head snapped around.

"He's gone on his *own?*"

Phillips gulped. "Aye, but I offered to go with him. There was no convincing him and he wanted us to stick together. If you're both right, every last one of them had a hand in it, and I don't much like those odds."

Anna fell silent. She could see the sense in that, but it didn't prevent her worrying for her husband, one lone man in the vast, snow-covered landscape.

"*He that is without sin among you, let him cast the first stone...*" MacKenzie said to herself, and thought of rocks that had fallen on Marcus Sage. "Frank, how many of those larger boulders did you find next to the body?"

"Five or six," he said softly.

There was a sudden rush of wind, and one of the mullioned windows flew open, followed by a crash. The window had knocked over a small vase, which had fallen to the floor. It had been empty, but its shards of porcelain had scattered into pieces, one of which lay half under the skirting board.

"Look," Anna said, pointing at it.

"That's funny," Phillips said. "There's no gap like that anywhere else in the room."

He walked over to pick it up, then ran his fingers around the small gap at the bottom, following it along and up to a slight dip in the wall.

"I think it's a door," he said.

The other two moved across to join him, and they pushed and prodded the wooden panelling until they found a tiny brass lever, almost invisible to the naked eye, and pulled it.

The narrow door swung open to reveal a hidden compartment, no more than the size of a broom cupboard, where Carole Black had in fact been keeping some of her household cleaning products. There was a jumbled assortment of dusters and bottles arranged on the shelves inside, but there was a lot more than that.

MacKenzie reached inside her pocket for the latex gloves she'd been keeping there, and snapped them on. Then, she reached up to grasp a black, leather-bound jotter set beside a packet of unused candles.

They took it to the table and flipped open the pages to the most recent entry:

Jacqui Baker (52)
Ran own restaurant until 2010, now works at call centre in Prudhoe. Widowed. Husband (Stuart) committed suicide by hanging, March 2011.

Rosie Baker (29)
Works as illustrator for graphic design company in Newcastle. Gave eulogy at father's funeral. No other information.

Nadia Halliwell (?)
Works as club spokesmodel in Newcastle. No other information.

Sheila Enfield (61) and David Enfield (64)
Inherited "Enfield's" gardening centre which she ran with husband (David). Went into administration late 2009, declared bankrupt. One son, Zachary (36), tree surgeon.

Marcus Sage (39)

Property developer since 2012. Owns or part-owns several clubs and restaurants in Newcastle and Durham. Formally changed name 1999. Previously known as 'Mark Dragfoot', address listed as Wallsend. Speak to Sharon at HMCTS for more details.

"Well, I know the first thing I'll be doing when we get back to the office," Phillips said. "Sharon from Her Majesty's Courts and Tribunals Service is going to feel my boot up her arse—"

"Never mind about that now, Frank. Marcus changed his name from 'Dragfoot'—that's what Carole used in the séance on Friday night, except she also said the name 'Elizabeth'. Obviously, those were the details he didn't want to come out, because they mustn't be common knowledge or publicly available."

"It's funny that the Bakers and the Enfields both lost their businesses around the same time," Anna said. "Didn't Samuel Black say they'd suffered financial loss, following a bad investment, too? Did he say when it happened?"

"No," Phillips said. "But I'll put money on it being around 2009."

"I just don't see how they're connected," MacKenzie muttered. "Marcus Sage changed his name a long time before any of these people lost their livelihoods."

"I wonder who Elizabeth was," Anna murmured.

CHAPTER 26

Ryan made it to *The Percy Arms* a few minutes before noon. The snow and the wind had been relentless, battering his body as he continued to put one foot in front of the other, all the while asking himself why the hell he couldn't have been an accountant, or a doctor, or *anything else* except a murder detective. However, his journey had been improved marginally by a set of antique snowshoes he'd found on display in the castle, no doubt belonging to some long-dead Arctic explorer.

"Back again, eh?" The landlord gave him a friendly wave as he stepped into the main bar. "On your own today?"

Ryan nodded, and hung his coat on a peg near the door. Despite having worn a hood, the snow had found its way beneath and his black hair was now dripping wet. He caught the bar towel Mike tossed him, and wiped the rest of the melting snow from his face and neck.

"Mike, I need to use your phone again—it's urgent."

Something in Ryan's tone must have transmitted itself, because the man nodded quickly and gestured towards the back office.

"Course, no bother. You know where it is. Get you anything?"

A snowplough, Ryan thought.

"No, thanks. I won't be long."

"Listen, mate—is there anything I should be worried about? What with you being CID...a few of us were wondering—it isn't anybody we know, is it?"

Of course, word travelled fast in small rural villages, and they would worry about their friends and neighbours. Technically, Next of Kin had been informed but, in Ryan's long experience, answering the first question generally encouraged further questions—none of which he presently had time to answer.

"I'm afraid I can't discuss any details at the moment," he said. "Everything is in hand, and I'm grateful for your cooperation."

He made directly for the telephone, noting the curious glances from the men and women gathered in the bar, who may very well have speculated about what had happened at the castle. The observant amongst them might have recognised the tall, serious policeman from past news reports, and it was both a comfort and a concern—a man like Ryan dealt only with the most serious offences, as a rule, which also meant there was nobody better qualified.

* * *

Lowerson answered his desk phone on the first ring.

"Jack, give me some good news."

"Well, Yates and I spent most of last night digging into the list you gave me, and it threw up some interesting facts about one of them, in particular. The man you were interested in, Marcus Sage? Well, I'd say your instincts are bang on."

"Tell me."

"Well, for starters, he's only been 'Marcus Sage' since 1999. Before then, he was Mark Dragfoot, born in Wallsend in 1980. In

2010, he was listed as one of several defendants in a class action for fraud, which went all the way to trial in the High Court. There were almost a hundred claimants in the litigation—"

"Let me guess," Ryan said. "They included the Bakers, the Enfields and the Blacks?"

At his desk, Lowerson grinned.

"You got it," he said. "That isn't to say they would have known about Sage, personally; they didn't all attend the trial, and his name was subsumed under the name of the corporate entity—Ariel Holdings Limited. It could be a coincidence."

"You know how I feel about coincidences, Jack."

"I know, I know—there's no such thing."

"You're damn right. One litigant being in the same place as the defendant is a bad coincidence, but six? What was the outcome of the case, incidentally?"

"It collapsed when the defendant company went into insolvent liquidation," Lowerson said. "The money was never recovered, and no restitution was ever made. People lost their homes, their businesses, their pensions and, in some cases, their lives."

Ryan thought of Jacqui Baker's husband.

"There's no such thing as a victimless crime," he murmured. "Anything else?"

"That isn't all," Lowerson said. "There was a juvenile file belonging to Mark Dragfoot, long before he tried his hand at defrauding people, sealed in 1996. Morrison rang The Powers That Be late last night, and we were given access to its contents about half an hour ago."

"Just in the nick of time."

"Yeah, and it makes for sad reading. When he was sixteen, Mark Dragfoot strangled a girl to death. She was his girlfriend at the time, and they went to the same school. The coroner ruled it 'death by misadventure', because they accepted Dragfoot's defence that the girl consented to being mildly asphyxiated during sex. Because he was found not guilty of manslaughter, his name was protected in the press. I guess he changed it because local people would still have known—and it's a pretty memorable name."

Ryan had been listening intently, as everything fell neatly into place. Now, he asked the most important question of all.

"What was the name of the girl, Jack?"

"Elizabeth, but she went by Lizzy. Lizzy Dodds."

Ryan closed his eyes, allowing himself a moment's grief on behalf of a father who had lost a daughter—but when he opened them again, they were hard and focused.

"Guess this means Sage was the one who killed Carole Black," Lowerson was saying. "Are you going to make the arrest and keep him under supervision until we can get up there?"

Ryan rubbed his temple to ease the ache, one he knew was more in his mind than in his body. "We found Marcus Sage dead at the bottom of the castle's oubliette, early this morning," he said.

Lowerson let out a long whistle. "Maybe a higher power intervened," he said, but knew Ryan would never accept that.

"Whoever killed Marcus took justice into their own hands," he said. "As much as they think he deserved it, as much as they wanted revenge, an eye for an eye is never the right way."

And Ryan would know. He had first-hand experience of what it was to lose a loved one to the hands of a depraved animal. He'd come as close as having his hands around the man's throat, so close he'd felt the blood beating frantically through his veins.

But it was not the right way.

And, in the end, perhaps a greater power had intervened, after all.

"If they did this—if they held their own kangaroo court and sentenced Marcus Sage, or Mark Dragfoot, to death—they flouted every moral code and every legal code we live by. That isn't justice, it's anarchy."

As he listened, Lowerson was reminded of why he'd always looked up to the man who was, he was proud to say, his boss, his friend and his greatest champion. There was no lack of compassion in Ryan; only a clear and unwavering understanding of an invisible line in the sand, and what it would mean for their shared world if people were given free rein to cross it.

"What can I do now?" he asked.

"I need you to get on to the Highways Authority, Mountain Rescue and any other organisation you can think of, Jack. I need reinforcements up at the castle, and I need them yesterday. I don't care if you have to come in on a bloody donkey, just make sure you get here by the end of the day."

"Consider it done," Lowerson replied, and then added, "Sir? You were only joking about the donkey part, weren't you?"

But the line had already gone dead.

CHAPTER 27

As the castle clock struck two, Ryan and his team joined the other occupants of the castle in the Great Hall one last time. A fire continued to crackle in the grate, burnishing their faces with a warm, ethereal glow so that—just for a moment—they seemed unreal. But then, the light shifted, and Sheila Enfield's voice rose up above all others.

"Well, Chief Inspector? Have you solved it, yet?"

Ryan gave her a tigerish smile.

"I think so, Mrs Enfield. I thought, perhaps, you might all like to hear our theory. Or, rather, *theories.*"

He stalked to the head of the long banqueting table, where they'd congregated over cups of tea and sandwiches, as though they hadn't a care in the world. Nadia was the only exception to this—she was sitting with her foot up on one of the occasional sofas. His eyes passed over each of them in turn, reading their body language, resting on Bill Dodds for long seconds before moving on.

"Are we all settled in? Good, because I have a Christmas ghost story for you, after all."

There were nervous glances around the table.

"Let's start at the beginning, with the murder of Carole Black," he said, and watched Dodds put a hand on his friend's shoulder.

"The circumstances of Mrs Black's death were puzzling, at first. I asked myself, how could anybody have murdered Carole, when there was only one set of footprints in the snow? Could our murderer fly? Of course not," he said. "Between us, we thought of every possible scenario, from crossbows to suicide, none of which seemed plausible. It wasn't until we considered what Mr Black had told us about Carole's predilection for playing practical jokes on her guests, that we realised the answer was glaringly obvious from the start."

"Was it?" Jacqui asked. "I'm afraid I still don't understand."

"We realised that Carole's killer had overheard the plan she'd discussed with her husband; a plan that relied on her making her way out to the south lawn, playing dead, and then screaming at exactly nine o'clock. Carole intended to lie dead and surprise whichever person found her first; it was an idea inspired by a real legend of a former lady of the house who was found outside on the lawn, stabbed with a letter knife. Unfortunately for Carole, the person who found her didn't jump in surprise, for they'd known all along they would find her alive and well. Instead of helping her up, they finished the job."

They looked amongst themselves, putting two and two together.

"You mean—*Mr Sage did it?*" Rosie squeaked. "But...he couldn't have...I mean, I ran out after him and he seemed so upset—"

"There was a time delay of around a minute before you joined him on the lawn," Ryan reminded her. "More than enough time for him to plunge a knife into her throat."

Rosie fell silent, thinking back.

"The knife handle was wet," she said, softly. "I wondered why it was wet."

"I have no proof of this yet, particularly as forensic testing has not been completed, but we believe Mr Sage used snow to wipe off his prints."

"Clever devil, wasn't he?" Sheila muttered.

"But why would he want to kill Carole?" Samuel asked, and all eyes turned at the sound of his quiet voice. "What had she ever done to him?"

This was a tricky part, Ryan thought. To try to bring forth a confession, it meant trampling over some things that might be held sacred.

But he had no choice.

"Were you aware, Mr Black, that Carole had a contact in the Courts Service, as well as a friend in the Passport Office, perhaps more that we don't yet know about, who were complicit in helping her to extort money from some of the guests who came to stay here?"

All the blood drained from Samuel's face.

"Now, just a minute, Ryan. You can't go around making accusations like that—" Dodds said, half rising from his chair.

"Sit down, please, Mr Dodds," he said, very softly. "I never make accusations I can't prove."

He turned to MacKenzie, who handed him the black leather jotter she had tucked inside a plastic bag.

"This is a personal record kept by Carole Black of every guest who stayed here in the past three years," he said. "It lists personal information, ages, addresses and significant others, but it also includes any deaths, marriages or significant life events. Occasionally, it includes prison records, and anything else available via an intensive internet search."

"Why?" Samuel said. "Why would she do that?"

"To take advantage of the castle's good reputation, and people who come to visit in good faith hoping to find genuine paranormal activity," Ryan said, simply. "Mr Black, you told me in your statement that you and Mrs Black had suffered a severe financial setback, owing to some bad investments. When was that?"

"I—it was back in 2009," he said.

"I don't believe any of this," Dodds stormed. "The poor woman's dead—murdered—and you're standing there giving a cold-blooded character assassination. It's a disgrace, and I would frankly have expected better of you, Ryan."

"Before the end of this discussion, I might just say the same of you," Ryan snapped, and Dodds faltered, his face turning hot and cold.

There, Ryan thought. *There was the truth, lurking beneath the surface.*

"Understanding why Carole died is the key to all the rest," Ryan explained. "It makes for hard hearing, but two people are dead. There has to be accountability."

"What if you never get accountability," Dodds muttered, and his eyes flashed fire. "What if the law fails, and you never get justice for your dead?"

"You fight, you lobby, you find peace," Ryan said, and the room looked on in awe as the two men entered into a battle of wills. "My sister was murdered. Did you know that?"

"No—I, didn't," Dodds confessed, suddenly on the back foot.

"She was murdered in front of me, and there wasn't a damn thing I could do about it. I had it in my grasp to kill the man who had killed her—and I almost did. But something stopped me. Not just my friend, DS Phillips," he said, nodding towards Frank. "It was the knowledge that, once you take a life, there's no going back. The knowledge of it lives in your heart and in your conscience forever. It haunts you—more so than any castle ghost."

Dodds looked crestfallen, as though he might break down at any moment, but then a voice interrupted them.

"You still haven't explained why Marcus killed Carole," Nadia said, quietly.

Ryan turned to find her sitting placidly on the sofa.

"You're right. Let me rectify that, now. We believe Carole was murdered because she found something out about Sage's past, something he didn't want ever to see the light of day. Normally, Carole used the information she discovered about people to inform her psychic readings and to add weight to the impression she could really commune with the spirits—as was sadly the case when she claimed to be speaking to your husband, Stuart."

He looked at Jacqui, whose lip wobbled as she reached for her daughter's hand.

"I knew it wasn't real," she whispered. "I knew it couldn't be."

Ryan nodded.

"Carole picked the wrong mark, when she picked Marcus Sage. You see, he wasn't always a successful property developer. At one time, he was young Mark Dragfoot, and he killed a girl called Elizabeth."

There were gasps around the room, and Bill Dodds dropped his head into his hands.

"It was ruled misadventure and his name was protected; the record sealed. Mark, or Marcus, went on with his life, while the girl's family were forced to live with their loss, and with the lies he probably told to undermine her credibility while she wasn't alive to defend herself."

Dodds looked directly ahead, at a space on the wall, but his mind was somewhere else entirely.

"You think Carole found out about this?" he asked, in a voice so low they strained to hear him. "You think she found out and tried to profit from it?"

Ryan nodded.

"Yes, I'm sorry."

Samuel shook his head, clearly shocked.

"I can't believe she would do that," he said. I—"

But he remembered how quickly they'd been able to pay off their debts. Just lately, it had seemed as though they were back on an even keel, and he'd noticed his wife wearing new clothes and even jewellery she couldn't account for.

It shamed him to think of how she might have come by it for, if what the detective said was true, that made her no better than the one who had cheated *them*.

"We believe that's why Carole died," Ryan continued. "In fact, we were readying ourselves to arrest Mr Sage when he turned up dead this morning."

Ryan paused.

"Which brings us on to the most puzzling problem of all."

CHAPTER 28

"As far as we can tell, there are three possible solutions to the problem of how Marcus Sage, the man formerly known as Mark Dragfoot, came to be found at the bottom of the oubliette."

The Great Hall was deathly quiet, with only the snapping of logs in the fire and the howling of the wind to break the silence.

"The first theory is that his death was a case of simple misadventure—which would be poetic, given his past exploits—and he took a tumble while he was walking around the castle late at night. A torch was found beside his body, which would support this theory. But then, there was other evidence to disprove it, such as the manner in which he fell, and the drag marks on the back of his heels. I suspect, once the pathologist examines his body, we'd find scuffing on his back, too."

"Why would he go out walking late at night?" Nadia protested. "I told you, I heard him answer a phone call—"

"That brings me on to my second theory," Ryan said. "When you told me about the call he'd taken, designed to lure him away from the safety of your apartment, this tallied with another feature of the crime scene. Namely, the larger pieces of bloodied rubble we found on and around his body, some having clearly connected with his face, others having only grazed his arms or legs. There were six of them."

He paused, looking around the table, counting each of them off in his head.

"When I spoke to my colleague, Detective Constable Lowerson, he told me the results of certain background checks I asked him to complete yesterday. The results were very revealing. He found that Mr Sage had, at one time, been listed as a defendant to a class action for fraud and embezzlement owing to the part he played in procuring money on behalf of Ariel Holdings Limited, which was a company incorporated in the British Virgin Islands. That case came to trial in 2010 and collapsed soon after, leaving over a hundred litigants severely out of pocket and, in some cases, ruined."

He watched the recognition flare in each of their faces, mingled with a degree of confusion.

"I was one of those people," Jacqui Baker said, and there were murmurs of agreement and nods around the table.

"Me too—"

"Yes, they took us for over fifty grand—"

Ryan held up his hands for quiet.

"There were six stones, and six of you sitting here whose names were listed on that action," he said. "Six of you who had reason to hate Marcus Sage. I can't imagine how sickening it must have been, to see him arrive here in his expensive car, swanning around the castle in clothes worth thousands of pounds, and not even to recognise any of you, or feel a moment's regret for what he had done."

"I swear, I didn't know it was him," Jacqui said, with every appearance of sincerity. "If I had, I wouldn't have been able to stay under the same roof—"

172

"But you had no choice," Ryan reminded her. "The snow trapped us all under the same roof, together, and gave some or all of you a once-in-a-lifetime opportunity to right a wrong, at least in your own eyes."

"I knew who he was," Sheila surprised them all by saying. "I recognised him straight away, *odious* man. But, if you think I'd sully my hands on that—that *vermin,* you're very mistaken."

"It's funny, isn't it, how you all jumped so easily to follow my colleague's advice to stay in the Great Hall after the oil ran out— or perhaps it didn't run out at all? Perhaps that was a good excuse to stay together, because so long as you remained close by, you could alibi one another."

"That's ridiculous," Samuel said. "Bill checked the oil himself."

"And stayed with you, throughout the night. Either one of you was free to go down to the oubliette and cast a stone, and each of you could claim you never left the apartment. Very neat, very tidy," Ryan said.

"That's not true," Rosie said, vehemently. "My mother and I don't have a murderous bone in our bodies. We wouldn't even think of it."

"Is that right? I wonder," Ryan said. "It would be natural to have felt a keen sense of injustice; to think of the father you lost, and who might still be here, were it not for Marcus Sage."

"No," Rosie sobbed. "*No!*"

There were loud protests around the room, from all but Bill Dodds, who continued to stare at the other side of the room, and Ryan hardened his heart. It gave him no pleasure at all, but he had to find the truth.

"Oh my God," Nadia said, tearfully. "I can see it now. I can *see* all of them crowding around, hurling stones at him…"

She dissolved into tears, which Ryan completely ignored.

"That brings me on to our third and final theory," he said, conversationally. "I neglected to say earlier that the full name of the unfortunate girl Marcus killed, back when he was Mark Dragfoot, was Elizabeth *Dodds*."

Sheila Enfield's mouth fell into a comical 'o'.

"She was your daughter, wasn't she, Bill?"

Dodds seemed to gather himself together, for he turned to Ryan with eyes that were no longer vacant and lost, but hard and resolute.

"Yes, she was."

There were more gasps around the room, and Samuel looked at his friend aghast.

"Bill?"

"You said this girl died when Marcus—or Mark—was only sixteen," Nadia said quickly, having recovered from her crying jag. "He'd look very different back then, wouldn't he? And he changed his name."

"That's true," Jacqui chimed in. "Honestly, I wouldn't have known him, and the case was only nine years ago."

Ryan turned to the Estate Manager.

"Did you recognise him, Bill?"

Dodds shook his head.

"I wouldn't have known him," he replied, and that was not quite a lie. It was true the man had changed beyond all recognition, and had a new name, too.

"But you knew who he was, didn't you, Bill? You knew, because you'd helped your accomplice to orchestrate this weekend, from the very beginning. You helped the person who found him, followed him, and studied what he liked to do, what kind of girls he preferred, and every other bit of his life. You issued the prize vouchers to the people you planned to blame, to people you knew had an axe to grind against him, and would therefore fall under suspicion."

"He was with me all night," Samuel said. "I'll swear to that."

"Yes," Ryan said. "I believe he *was* with you all night, establishing his own alibi, once he'd ensured that his accomplice had a solid alibi too."

"I—I don't understand," David Enfield said. "Are you saying he did, or he didn't kill Marcus Sage?"

"He may not have dealt the killing blow, but he was a full accomplice," Ryan said. "I suspect he might also have come up with the original idea. Did you, Bill? When was it? When Carole and Samuel told you they'd lost out to Ariel Holdings, and mentioned some of the names of the people involved? Did you recognise the man you'd followed all these years, and start to concoct a plan?"

"But who—?" Sheila started to say, and then her eyes slid across the room to the young woman sitting on the sofa, so serenely.

"Yes," Ryan said.

Sheila scoffed. "You must be mad. Nadia couldn't have walked three paces, let alone killed a man and dragged him through the castle!"

"She didn't have any injury when she did that," Ryan said softly.

Those seated around the table rose up again in her defence, and he held up his hands before walking over to stand next to Nadia, who looked up at him in defiance.

"Go on, Chief Inspector. You were telling everybody how I must have scampered through the castle on a broken ankle," she said. "I'm sure we're all dying to hear the rest."

Ryan's eyes remained unflinching.

"When you screamed last night, it struck me as odd that it came just as the clock was chiming seven. Carole and Samuel used the clock as a kind of stage cue, if you like, to let one another know the game was afoot. I think you did the same thing—you, and your father—to make sure you had an airtight alibi."

"*Father?*" Sheila cried, and turned to Bill in accusation, as if that were a juicy bit of gossip he ought to have shared sooner.

"Yes, Nadia is my daughter—but we've been estranged for years," he said, and almost sounded sincere.

"No," Ryan said. "But that's the story you agreed to tell. The truth is, Nadia is Lizzy's younger sister. She grew up in the shadow of her loss, overhearing all your hatred, your anger and, most of all, your pain."

He turned to her and saw the family similarities, now he was looking for them.

"It was you, Nadia, who thought of growing close to Marcus—you sacrificed your body for the greater good, as you saw it. Isn't that right?"

She remained silent, but she swallowed the bile that rose up in her throat as she remembered Marcus's skin touching hers.

"You got a job in one of his clubs, and made sure he noticed you. You didn't care how long it would take. Eventually, you succeeded, and it was time for your father to issue the prize vouchers."

"Wait a minute," David said. "Even if she's his daughter, I still don't see how she could have done a thing on that ankle of hers."

Ryan turned to him and asked a simple question.

"Who found Nadia, at the bottom of the stairs?"

David swung around to look at Bill, who was seated directly opposite.

"But…we saw it. I mean, she was in agony. Wasn't she?"

He turned back to Ryan, who shook his head and looked back at Nadia.

"She's a good actress," he said. "Consider the chiming of the clock. A few minutes before seven, Bill excused himself to make a start on bringing up the electric heaters, or so he said. But when I spoke to my colleagues who were at the table, they told me it was strange that he seemed in such a rush, considering he'd barely finished his dinner."

Ryan lifted a shoulder.

"Bill couldn't miss his cue," he said. "It was imperative he should be the first to find Nadia, and the first to bandage her up. Marcus wouldn't know any better—he didn't care for Nadia at all, and certainly wouldn't bother to check her bandage to see if there was any real damage. Imagine his shock, in the early hours of the morning, when she clubbed him over the back of his head and dragged him through the castle to the place both she and her father felt he truly belonged."

Ryan stuck his hands in his pockets.

"After that, it was a question of good stage management, wasn't it?" he asked Nadia, who continued to stare at him with silent venom. "You'd already brought some of that wall down, hadn't you, Bill?"

Ryan moved back across to look at the Estate Manager.

"A wall that had stood for eight hundred years or more suddenly decided to crumble. That's odd, don't you think?" he asked the room at large. "But very convenient for their purposes. Bill chipped away seven neat pieces of stone—he'd counted Carole in the number originally, you see," he added, for Samuel's benefit. "But, in the end, only six were needed to complete the staging. I found the seventh stone slotted loosely back into the wall."

In the heavy silence that followed, even Sheila Enfield was rendered momentarily speechless.

Then, there came three loud claps from the direction of the sofa. Ryan turned to find Nadia smiling at him with an air of complacency he found highly distasteful.

"Well, I think it's clear that being stuck inside these castle walls has had a very strange effect on your mind, Chief Inspector," she said. "For one thing, you don't have a single shred of evidence for any of your little theories. Do you?"

Nadia looked towards the others in appeal.

"Yes, Elizabeth was my sister, but it was a very long time ago. I never like to think of it, and I was as shocked as you when I heard Carole say her name at the séance. I said nothing, because I wanted to speak to my father about it, and to ask how she could have known. Then, when Carole died, I was afraid. We both were. I started to think—" Her voice broke. "I started to think that the man I'd met at the club in Newcastle was the very same man who'd killed my big sister, all those years before. I was horrified...I felt sick...I—"

"Rubbish," Ryan snapped.

"But it's what I'll tell the jury," she whispered, so that only he might hear.

Ryan laughed.

"I'll take my chances," he said. "You say there's no evidence, and that it's all an awful coincidence that your lives were intertwined, together, here at Chillingham?" He shook his head. "The forensics team will be here, soon. I'll make sure that *no stone goes unturned*. Every bedsheet, every scrap of carpet and curtain will be tested, until I find whatever was used to immobilise him in the early hours of this morning. Did you remember to push the phone handset into Marcus's hand to support your story about him receiving a phone call? It's going to look mighty suspicious if none of his DNA is found on the handset."

Nadia stared straight ahead, as if her face were set in stone, so Ryan continued. "The Digital Forensics team will seize your laptop, your mobile, as well as every other tech device from your home and here at the castle, until they trace who was responsible for sending those prize vouchers."

"You'll never—it won't—Dad?"

She appealed to her father and, in his peripheral vision, Ryan saw Bill Dodds move to get up.

"It was me—I killed him. Nadia had nothing to do with it. You have to—"

"Tell it to the jury," Ryan said quietly. "It's over."

* * *

As the tractor lumbered over deep snowdrifts in the northernmost part of Northumberland, Detective Constable Jack Lowerson reflected that, if he hadn't chosen to be a detective, farming would have been a very pleasant way of life. His friend, Oliver, was President of the Northumberland Federation of Young Farmers, and one phone call was all it had taken to assemble a convoy of farm vehicles to clear a pathway through the snow, all the way from the A1 to Chillingham. It had taken hours to get there, and his feet were frozen solid, but as they arrived at the bottom of the gates leading up to the castle and saw the snow blocking their entry, he knew they'd arrived not a moment too soon.

Glancing back, he gave the thumbs-up signal to three police jeeps, which followed in the tracks made by the industrial farm vehicle fitted with a makeshift snowplough.

"Can I honk the horn?"

The farmer rolled his eyes. "Aye, go on then."

Lowerson gave a generous tug on the horn and, a couple of minutes later, spotted Ryan waving from one of the upper windows.

"The cavalry's arrived!"

EPILOGUE

Christmas Eve

The Christmas tree twinkled in the late afternoon twilight, while Bing Crosby dreamed about a white Christmas on the kitchen radio. The smell of roasting chestnuts carried on the air as Phillips made his 'famous' stuffing, to be used exclusively for the turkey stotties he intended to dish out on Boxing Day. There was laughter on the air, something too often in short supply, and a renewed gratitude for the friends and family they held dear, especially after their recent experience. Ryan might not have been religious, but he'd always thought that the festive season was a time for family. Since Phillips, MacKenzie and Samantha were, in all ways, like family to him, he could think of no reason why they shouldn't spend the time together.

Which was why his eyes were now being assaulted by the sight of Phillips in a reindeer hat, and why Samantha was beating him for the second time that evening at Monopoly.

"Why do you always have to be the banker?" he queried, suspiciously.

"Because it's a good way for me to practice my addition and subtraction," the little girl replied, with wide, innocent green eyes. "It's mostly a game of chance, you know."

Ryan shook his head, and handed over the last of his hundreds after landing on Mayfair for the third time in a row.

"Do you take IOUs?" he asked.

"No, but I can be persuaded to offer you a discount in exchange for one of those little gold chocolates you've got hanging on the tree," Samantha said, with a hopeful expression.

Ryan looked past her to check whether MacKenzie and Phillips were listening, then pointed a finger.

"Now, look, kid. You've already had two of those, and it's nearly dinnertime."

"Better pay up, then," she said, with a sad little shrug.

"You're a hard-headed woman of business," he chuckled.

"You'd better believe it."

Anna watched their exchange from her position on the sofa and smiled at the sight of her husband, always so strong for others, enjoying a well-earned moment of calm.

Later, when the game was over and Samantha had trotted off to the kitchen to forage for snacks, Ryan put the game away and came to sit beside his wife.

"How are you doing?" he asked. "You seem a bit quiet. Is everything alright?"

"Everything's fine," she said, and touched her lips to his. "I was considering giving you an early Christmas present, that's all."

He raised an eyebrow. "That sounds promising."

She chuckled, and then rose to walk over to the tree, where she'd wrapped a last-minute addition to his small pile of gifts. She held it in her hands for a moment, then walked back to hand it to him.

"Merry Christmas," she said.

Ryan frowned, hearing an odd note to her voice, but turned his attention to the unassuming rectangular object he held in his hands. If he were to guess, he'd say it was a book, and he wondered why she was looking at him with such expectation.

Perhaps…

The wrapping fell away and he found himself looking down at a paperback entitled, *A Guide to Parenting for First Time Mums and Dads.*

He looked up and into her deep brown eyes, which were glowing.

"Are you sure?" he whispered.

Anna nodded.

"We don't know what the future holds, especially after the troubles I've had before, but…yes, I'm sure. The baby's due in early summer."

Ryan gave her one of the smiles he reserved only for her; the kind that spread all the way to his eyes.

"I love you," he said deeply, and drew her into his arms. "I love both of you."

Anna laughed happily.

"We love you too."

* * *

When the others in the kitchen heard a sudden burst of laughter as Ryan danced his wife around the Christmas tree in time to the music, MacKenzie and Phillips looked at one another and then back at Samantha.

"Come on, you two. A deal's a deal."

There were grumbles, but then her parents grudgingly handed over two shiny fifty-pence pieces.

"Told you she was going to have a baby," Samantha said, happily. "But nobody ever listens to kids."

"Smarty-pants," Phillips said, with a touch of pride.

"Double or nothing, it's a boy," MacKenzie said.

"Oh, you're on."

DCI Ryan will return in 2020

If you would like to be kept up to date with new releases from LJ Ross, please complete an e-mail contact form on her Facebook page or website, www.ljrossauthor.com.

If you enjoy the DCI Ryan Mysteries, why not try the new series by LJ Ross:

THE ALEXANDER GREGORY THRILLERS?

Read on at the end of this book for an exclusive sneak peak at IMPOSTOR—book #1 in the new series—which is available in all good bookshops right now!

AUTHOR'S NOTE

Many readers over the past five years have requested that I write a fun Christmas story for DCI Ryan & Co., but until now I've never quite found the time or opportunity to do so. However, I'd always imagined an opening scene where he and the gang become lost in the snow, because this is something that happened to my husband and me, as we were driving home one winter with our three-month-old baby son in the back seat of our car. We'd been visiting his grandfather in Perth, who hadn't been well for a long time, and it was important to us that he should meet his grandson sooner rather than later. It was a lovely day, and one I will always remember, but the journey home was dreadful. We were diverted off the A1, much the same as Ryan and his friends were in this story, and we found ourselves in unfamiliar territory without the usual access to the outside world. The snowy diversion was an endless, winding road over hill and vale, under cover of darkness and in icy conditions. I knew the same fear that Anna experienced, because we truly felt lost in the wilderness.

But then, that's the beauty of Northumberland! It's a wild, rugged place where it's possible to stumble upon an ancient castle quite unexpectedly. In fact, when I considered which castle might be the perfect setting for this story, I could think of none better than Chillingham. It's a magical place, and I would heartily recommend that you visit it, if you can. The castle is privately owned but open to the public, and you can stay overnight. There is an oubliette, a dungeon and many of the other things mentioned in this book—but certain aspects have, naturally, been altered to fit my fictional tale of murder and mayhem. The most obvious of these is that none of my characters are based on real people, either living or dead. All of the real staff at the castle are very charming and extremely knowledgeable about the land and its history, which is very impressive. My thanks to them for the fun ghost tour, as well—for those who don't know, Chillingham is indeed reputed to be the most haunted castle in England, so if you enjoy the paranormal, it's a 'must-see' place!

My thanks must also go to you, Dear Reader. A significant portion of the proceeds of this book will be going towards charity ventures; specifically, the Lindisfarne Reading Challenge, a new literacy scheme I have founded, which is designed to benefit children from the most disadvantaged backgrounds. My hope is that we can continue to do our bit to close the 'disadvantage gap' between children, and this is one small initiative in that wider goal I am sure we all share: namely, to create a society we can be proud of—or, as DS Phillips would put it, to make sure there's enough bacon stotties for all.

As a final remark, I'm aware that this story is shorter than some readers will be used to. It's longer than a novella, but not as long as my usual novels—although, incidentally, it's about the same length as the average Agatha Christie (did you know they're generally 40–60,000 words?). What should we call it, then? Perhaps we could think of this book as a Christmas pudding: a bit smaller, a bit sweeter, but very filling!

I hope you enjoy reading it, and Happy Holidays to all of you.

LJ ROSS

December 2019

ABOUT THE AUTHOR

LJ Ross is an international bestselling author, best known for creating atmospheric mystery and thriller novels, including the DCI Ryan series of Northumbrian murder mysteries which have sold over four million copies worldwide.

Her debut, *Holy Island*, was released in January 2015 and reached number one in the UK and Australian charts. Since then, she has released a further sixteen novels, all of which have been top three global bestsellers and thirteen of which have been UK #1 bestsellers. Louise has garnered an army of loyal readers through her storytelling and, thanks to them, several of her books reached the coveted spot whilst only available to pre-order ahead of release.

Louise was born in Northumberland, England. She studied undergraduate and postgraduate Law at King's College, University of London and then abroad in Paris and Florence. She spent much of her working life in London, where she was a lawyer for a number of years until taking the decision to change career and pursue her dream to write. Now, she writes full time and lives with her husband and son in Northumberland. She enjoys reading all manner of books, travelling and spending time with family and friends.

If you enjoyed *Ryan's Christmas*, please consider leaving a review online.

If you would like to be kept up to date with new releases from LJ Ross, please complete an e-mail contact form on her Facebook page or website, www.ljrossauthor.com.

IMPOSTOR

– AN ALEXANDER GREGORY THRILLER

LJ Ross

PROLOGUE

August 1987

She was muttering again.

The boy heard it from beneath the covers of his bed; an endless, droning sound, like flies swarming a body. The whispering white noise of madness.

Poor, poor baby, she was saying. *My poor, poor baby.*

Over and over she repeated the words, as her feet paced the hallway outside his room. The floorboards creaked as she moved back and forth, until her footsteps came to an abrupt halt.

He hunkered further down, wrapping his arms around his legs, as if the pattern of Jedi knights on his *Star Wars* duvet cover could protect him.

It couldn't.

The door swung open and his mother was silhouetted in its frame, fully dressed despite it being the middle of the night. She strode across the room and shook his coiled body with an unsteady hand.

"Wake up! We need to go to the hospital."

The boy tried not to sigh. She didn't like it when he sighed, when he looked at her the 'wrong' way, or when he argued. Even if he did, she wouldn't listen.

She wouldn't even *hear*.

"I'm awake," he mumbled, although his body was crying out for sleep.

He was always sleepy.

"Come on, get dressed," she continued, and he tried not to look directly at her as she scurried about the room, pulling out clothes at random for him to wear. He didn't want to see her eyes, or what was hidden behind them. They'd be dark again, like they were before, and they'd look straight through him.

There came a soft moan from the bedroom next door, and his mother hurried out, leaving him to pull on jeans and a faded *Power Rangers* t-shirt. The clock on the bedside table told him it was three-seventeen a.m., in cheerful neon-green light. If he had the energy to spare, he might have wondered whether the children he'd seen playing in the garden next door ever got sick, like he did, or whether they got to go to school.

He remembered going to school, once.

He remembered liking it.

But his mother said he was too ill to go to school now, and he'd learn so much more at home, where she could take care of him and Christopher.

It wasn't her fault that, despite all her care, neither boy seemed to get any better.

Once, when she thought he was asleep, she'd come in to sit on the edge of his bed. She'd stroked a hand over his hair and told him that she loved him. For a moment, he thought Mummy had come back; but then, she'd moved her mouth close to his ear and told him it was all because Daddy had left them to be with something called a Filthy Whore, and everything would have been alright if he'd never gone away. He hadn't known what she meant. At first, he'd wondered if some kind of galactic monster had lured his father away. Maybe, at this very moment, he was trapped in a cast of bronze, just like Han Solo.

She called his name, and the boy dragged his skinny body off the bed. There was no time to make up fairy tales about his father, or to wonder how other children lived.

Or how they died.

* * *

There was more muttering at the hospital.

He could hear it, beyond the turquoise curtain surrounding his hospital bed. Whenever somebody passed by, the material rippled on the wind and he caught sight of the serious-looking doctors and nurses gathered a short distance away.

"*I can't see any medical reason—*" he heard one of them say, before the curtain flapped shut again. "*This needs to be reported.*"

"*There have been cases,*" another argued.

"*One dead already, the youngest in critical condition—*"

The boy tensed as he recognised the quick *slap-slap-slap* of his mother's tread against the linoleum floor.

"Where's my son? Where've you taken him?" she demanded, in a shrill voice. "Is he in there?"

He saw her fingers grasp the edge of the curtain, and unconsciously shrank back against the pillows, but she did not pull it back.

There ensued a short argument, conducted in professional undertones.

"If you really think—alright. Yes, yes, he can stay overnight, so long as I stay with him at all times. But what about Christopher?"

The voices receded back down the corridor as they moved towards the High Dependency Unit, where his younger brother lay against scratchy hospital bedsheets, fighting for his life.

* * *

When the boy awoke the next morning, he was not alone.

Three people surrounded his bed. One, he recognised as the doctor who'd snuck him a lollipop the previous night, and she gave him a small smile. Another was a stern-faced man wearing a dark suit that reminded him of his father, and the other was a young woman in a rumpled police uniform with sad brown eyes.

"Hi, there," the doctor said. "How're you doing, champ?"

There was a false note of cheer to her voice that made him nervous.

"W-where's my mum?"

The three adults exchanged an uncomfortable glance.

"You'll see your mother soon," the man told him. "I'm afraid she's had some bad news. You both have."

In careful, neutral tones, they spoke of how his younger brother had died during the night and, with every passing word, the boy's pale, ghostly-white face became more shuttered.

It had happened before, you see.

Last year, his baby sister had died too, before she'd reached her first birthday.

He remembered all the cards and flowers arriving at the house they used to live in; the endless stream of neighbours pouring into his mother's living room to condole and glean a little gossip about their misfortune. He remembered his mother's arm wrapped around his shoulder, cloying and immoveable, like a band of steel.

"*These two are all I have left, now,*" she'd said, tearfully, drawing Christopher tightly against her other side. "*I can only pray that God doesn't take them, too.*"

And, while the mourners tutted and wept and put 'a little something' in envelopes to help out, he'd watched his mother's eyes and wondered why she was so happy.

CHAPTER 1

Ballyfinny
County Mayo, Ireland
Thirty years later

"**D**addy, what's an '*eejit*?'"

Liam Kelly exited the roundabout—where he'd recently been cut-up by the aforementioned *eejit* driving a white Range Rover—and rolled his eyes. His three-year-old daughter was growing bigger every day, and apparently her ears were, too.

"That's just a word to describe somebody who…ah, does silly things."

She thought about it.

"Are you an *eejit*, Daddy?"

Liam roared with laughter and smiled in the rear-view mirror.

"It's been said," he admitted, with a wink. "Nearly home now, sugarplum. Shall we tell Mammy all about how well you did in your swimming class, today?"

His daughter grinned and nodded.

"I swam like a fish, didn't I?"

"Aye, you did. Here we are."

It took a minute for him to unbuckle her child seat and to collect their bags, but then Liam and his daughter were skipping hand in hand up the short driveway leading to the front door of their bungalow on the outskirts of the town. It was perched on higher ground overlooking the lough and, though it had been a stretch to buy the place, he was reminded of why they had each time he looked out across the sparkling water.

The front door was open, and they entered the hallway with a clatter of footsteps.

"We're back!" he called out.

But there was not a whisper of sound on the air, and he wondered if his wife was taking a nap. The first trimester was always tiring.

"Maybe Mammy's having a lie-down," he said, and tapped a finger to his lips. "Let's be quiet like mice, alright?"

"Okay," she replied, in a stage whisper.

"You go along and play in your bedroom and I'll bring you a glass of milk in a minute," he said, and smiled as she tiptoed down the corridor with exaggerated care.

When the little girl pushed open the door to her peaches-and-cream bedroom, she didn't notice her mother at first, since she was lying so serenely amongst the stuffed toys on the bed. When she did, she giggled, thinking of the story of Goldilocks.

"You're in my bed!" she whispered.

She crept towards her mother, expecting her eyes to open at any moment.

But they didn't.

The little girl began to feel drowsy after her exertions at the swimming pool, and decided to curl up beside her. She clambered onto the bed and, when her hands brushed her mother's cold skin, she tugged her rainbow blanket over them both.

"That's better," she mumbled, as her eyelids drooped.

When Liam found them lying there a short while later, the glass fell from his nerveless hand and shattered to the floor at his feet. There was a ringing in his ears, the pounding of blood as his body fought to stay upright. He wanted to scream, to shout—to reject the truth of what lay clearly before him.

But there was his daughter to think of.

"C-come here, baby," he managed, even as tears began to fall. "Let's—let's leave Mammy to sleep."

CHAPTER 2

South London
One month later

Doctor Alexander Gregory seated himself in one of the easy chairs arranged around a low coffee table in his office, then nodded towards the security liaison nurse who hovered in the doorway.

"I'll take it from here, Pete."

The man glanced briefly at the other occupant in the room, then stepped outside to station himself within range, should his help be required.

After the door clicked shut, Gregory turned his attention to the woman seated opposite. Cathy Jones was in her early sixties but looked much younger; as though life's cares had taken very little toll. Her hair was dyed and cut into a snazzy style by a mobile hairdresser who visited the hospital every few weeks. She wore jeans and a cream wool jumper, but no jewellery—as per the rules. Her fingernails were painted a daring shade of purple and she had taken time with her make-up, which was flawless. For all the world, she could have been one of the smart, middle-aged women he saw sipping rosé at a wine bar in the city, dipping focaccia bread into small bowls of olive oil and balsamic while they chatted with their friends about the latest episode of *Strictly Come Dancing*.

That is, if she hadn't spent much of the past thirty years detained under the Mental Health Act.

"It's nice to see you again, Cathy. How was your week?"

They went through a similar dance every Thursday afternoon, where he asked a series of gentle, social questions to put her at ease, before attempting to delve into the deeper ones in accordance with her care plan. Though he was generally optimistic by nature, Gregory did not hold out any great hope that, after so long in the system, the most recent strategy of individual and group sessions, art and music therapy, would bring this woman any closer to re-entering normal society—but he had to try.

Cathy leaned forward suddenly, her eyes imploring him to listen.

"I wanted to speak to you, Doctor," she said, urgently. "It's about the next review meeting."

"Your care plan was reviewed recently," he said, in an even tone. "Don't you remember?"

There was a flicker of frustration, quickly masked.

"The clinical team made a mistake," she said.

"Oh? What might that be?"

Gregory crossed one leg lightly over the other and reached for his notepad, ready to jot down the latest theory she had cobbled together to explain the reason for her being there in the first place. In thirty years as a patient in four different secure hospitals, under the care of numerous healthcare professionals, Cathy had never accepted the diagnosis of her condition.

Consequently, she hadn't shown a scrap of remorse for her crimes, either.

"Well, I was reading only the other day about that poor, *poor* mother whose baby died. You know the one?"

Gregory did. The tragic case of Sudden Infant Death Syndrome had been widely reported in the press, but he had no intention of sating this woman's lust for tales of sensational child-deaths.

"Anyway, all those years ago, when they put me in *here*, the doctors didn't know so much about cot death. Not as much as they do now. If they had, things might have been different—"

Gregory looked up from his notepad, unwilling to entertain the fantasies that fed her illness.

"Do you remember the reason the pathologist gave for the deaths of your daughter, Emily, and your son, Christopher? Neither of them died following Sudden Infant Death Syndrome, as I think you're well aware."

The room fell silent, and she stared at him with mounting hatred, which he studiously ignored. Somewhere behind the reinforced glass window, they heard the distant buzz of a security gate opening.

"It was a cover up," she said, eventually. "You doctors are all the same. You always cover for each other. My children were *ill*, and not one of those quacks knew what to do about it—"

Gregory weighed up the usefulness of fishing out the pathology reports completed in 1987 following the murders of a two-year-old boy and a girl of nine months.

Not today.

"I'm going to appeal the court ruling," she declared, though every one of her previous attempts had failed. "You know what your problem is, Doctor? You've spent so long working with crackpots, you can't tell when a sane person comes along."

She'd tried this before, too. It was a favourite pastime of hers, to try to beat the doctor at his own game. It was a classic symptom of Munchausen's syndrome by proxy that the sufferer developed an obsessive interest in the medical world, and its terminology. Usually, in order to find the best way to disguise the fact they were slowly, but surely, killing their own children.

"How did it make you feel, when your husband left you, Cathy?"

Gregory nipped any forthcoming tirade neatly in the bud, and she was momentarily disarmed. Then, she gave an ugly laugh.

"Back to that old chestnut again, are we?"

When he made no reply, she ran an agitated hand through her hair.

"How would any woman feel?" she burst out. "He left me with three children, for some *tart* with cotton wool for brains. I was well rid of him."

But her index finger began to tap against the side of the chair.

Tap, tap, tap.

Tap, tap, tap.

"When was the divorce finalised, Cathy?"

"It's all there in your bloody file, isn't it?" she spat. "Why bother to ask?"

"I'm interested to know if you remember."

"Sometime in 1985," she muttered. "January, February…Emily was only a couple of months old. The bastard was at it the whole time I was pregnant."

"That must have been very hard. Why don't you tell me about it?"

Her eyes skittered about the room, all of her previous composure having evaporated.

"There's nothing to tell. He buggered off to Geneva to live in a bloody great mansion with his Barbie doll, while I was left to bring up his children. He barely even called when Emily was rushed into hospital. When *any* of them were."

"Do you think their…*illness*, would have improved, if he had?"

She gave him a sly look.

"How could it have made a difference? They were suffering from very rare conditions, outside our control."

Gregory's lips twisted, but he tried again.

"Did a part of you hope that news of their 'illness' might have encouraged your husband to return to the family home?"

"I never thought of it," she said. "All of my thoughts and prayers were spent trying to save my children."

He glanced up at the large, white plastic clock hanging on the wall above her head.

It was going to be a long morning.

* * *

An hour after Gregory finished his session with Cathy, he had just finished typing up his notes when a loud siren began to wail.

He threw open the door to his office and ran into the corridor, where the emergency alarm was louder still, echoing around the walls in a cacophony of sound. He took a quick glance in both directions and spotted a red flashing light above the doorway of one of the patients' rooms. He sprinted towards it, dimly aware of running footsteps following his own as others responded to whatever awaited them beyond the garish red light.

The heels of his shoes skidded against the floor as he reached the open doorway, where he found one of the ward nurses engaged in a mental battle with a patient who had fashioned a rudimentary knife from a sharpened fragment of metal and was presently holding it against her own neck.

Gregory reached for the alarm button and, a moment later, the wailing stopped. In the residual silence, he took a deep breath and fell back on his training.

"Do you mind if I come in?" he asked, holding out his hands, palms outstretched in the universal gesture for peace.

He exchanged a glance with the nurse, who was holding up well. He'd never ascribed to old-school hierarchies within hospital walls; doctors were no better equipped to deal with situations of this kind than an experienced mental health nurse—in fact, the reverse was often true. Life at Southmoor High Security Psychiatric Hospital followed a strict routine, for very good reason. Depending on their level of risk, patients were checked at least every fifteen minutes to try to prevent suicide attempts being made, even by those who had shown no inclination before, or who had previously been judged 'low risk'.

Especially those.

There were few certainties in the field of mental healthcare, but uncertainty was one of them.

"I'd like you to put the weapon down, Hannah," he said, calmly. "It's almost lunchtime, and it's Thursday. You know what that means."

As he'd hoped, she looked up, her grip on the knife loosening a fraction.

"Jam roly-poly day," he smiled. It was a mutual favourite of theirs and, in times of crisis, he needed to find common ground.

Anything to keep her alive.

"Sorry, Doc," she whispered, and plunged the knife into her throat…

IMPOSTOR is available in all good bookshops right now!

Printed in Great Britain
by Amazon